The perfect pitch?

Michael took a deep breath, aimed, and let his fastball fly. The hitter was ready for it, eager for anything he could reach out for, and he lunged after the fastball like a golfer.

"Strike two!" the umpire called. Michael snapped the ball back in his glove and nodded to Carlos. They had the guy on the ropes. He peered in for the sign.

Carlos dropped two fingers.

The curveball? Was Carlos crazy? A third of the time it bounced to the plate, and a third of the time it floated in like the fattest, most hittable pitch the batter had ever seen. Sure, there was that other third of the time when it broke just right, but there was no way he could take that chance. He shook Carlos off.

Carlos's catcher's mask tilted sideways, and Michael knew he was wondering: "If not now, when?"

Michael sighed again. Carlos was right, and he knew it. He motioned for Carlos to cycle through the pitches one more time and nodded at the sign for curveball.

"Drop in there," Michael whispered as he went into his windup. "Drop in there drop in there drop in there."

He released, staring the ball down as it flew closer, closer, closer—

Other Books by Alan Gratz

Samurai Shortstop

Something Rotten

Something Wicked

THE BROOKLYN NINE

A Novel in Nine Innings

by Alan Gratz

speak

An Imprint of Penguin Group (USA) Inc.

SPEAK

Published by the Penguin Group

Penguin Group (USA) Inc., 345 Hudson Street, New York, New York 10014, U.S.A.

Penguin Group (Canada), 90 Eglinton Avenue East, Suite 700, Toronto, Ontario, Canada M4P 2Y3
(a division of Pearson Penguin Canada Inc.)

Penguin Books Ltd, 80 Strand, London WC2R 0RL, England

Penguin Ireland, 25 St Stephen's Green, Dublin 2, Ireland (a division of Penguin Books Ltd)

Penguin Group (Australia), 250 Camberwell Road, Camberwell, Victoria 3124, Australia
(a division of Pearson Australia Group Pty Ltd)

Penguin Books India Pvt Ltd, 11 Community Centre, Panchsheel Park, New Delhi - 110 017, India

Penguin Group (NZ), 67 Apollo Drive, Rosedale, North Shore 0632, New Zealand
(a division of Pearson New Zealand Ltd)

Penguin Books (South Africa) (Pty) Ltd, 24 Sturdee Avenue,
Rosebank, Johannesburg 2196, South Africa

Registered Offices: Penguin Books Ltd, 80 Strand, London WC2R 0RL, England

First published in the United States of America by Dial Books,
a member of Penguin Group (USA) Inc., 2009
Published by Speak, an imprint of Penguin Group (USA) Inc., 2010

17 19 20 18 16

THE LIBRARY OF CONGRESS HAS CATALOGED THE DIAL BOOKS EDITION AS FOLLOWS:
Gratz, Alan, date.
The Brooklyn nine : a novel in nine innings / by Alan Gratz.
p. cm.
Summary: Follows the fortunes of a German immigrant family through nine generations,
beginning in 1845, as they experience American life and play baseball.
ISBN 978-0-8037-3224-7 (hc)
[1. Baseball—History—Fiction. 2. United States—History—Fiction.] I. Title.
PZ7.G77224Br 2009 [Fic]—dc22 2008021263

Speak ISBN 978-0-14-241544-3

Designed by Nancy R. Leo-Kelly
Text set in Adobe Garamond

Printed in the United States of America

For Mom and Dad, finally

THE BROOKLYN NINE

First Inning: Play Ball

Manhattan, New York, 1845

1

Nine months ago, Felix Schneider was the fastest boy in Bremen, Germany. Now he was the fastest boy in Manhattan, New York. He was so fast, in fact, the ship that had brought him to America arrived a day early.

Now he stood on first base, waiting to run.

"Put the poreen just about here, ya rawney Dutchman!" the Striker called. English was difficult enough for Felix to understand, and almost unintelligible when spoken by the Irish. But the "Dutchman" at Feeder—another German boy like Felix—didn't need to understand Cormac's words to know where he wanted him to throw the ball. He lobbed it toward the plate and the Irish boy slapped the ball to the right side beyond first base.

Felix ran full out. His legs churned in the soft mud, but his shoes gave him traction, propelling him toward second base. He was a racehorse, a locomotive. The world was a blur when he ran, and he could feel his blood thumping through his veins like the steam pistons pounding out a rhythm on the fast ferry to Staten Island. Felix flew past the parcel that stood for second base and dug for third.

"Soak him!" one of the boys called. Felix glanced over his shoulder just in time to see an English boy hurl the baseball at him. He danced out of the way and the ball sailed past him, missing his vest by less than an inch. Felix laughed and charged on to third, turning on the cap there and heading for home.

"Soak the bloody devil!" one of the other Irish boys cried. The ball came at Felix again, but this time the throw was well wide. He pounced on the rock at home plate with both feet and celebrated the point.

"Ace!" Felix cried. "Ace, ace, ace!"

"No it weren't," called one of the buckwheats, a boy just back from the Ohio territory. "You missed second base!"

Felix ran straight to second base to argue, and was met there by the boys on both teams.

"You're out, ya plonker!" said one of the Irish boys.

"The heck I was!" said Felix. He stepped forward to challenge him, and the boy laughed.

"You sure you want to get them fancy ones and twos there muddy, Dutchman?"

He was on again about Felix's shoes, which were better than everyone else's. Felix's father, a cobbler, had made them for him—sturdy brown leather lace-ups with good thick heels. They were the only thing he still had to remind him of his family back in Bremen.

The boys looked down at Felix's shoes. That's when they all saw Felix's footprints in the wet earth. He'd missed second base by a foot.

"Three out, all out," the buckwheat said.

Felix snatched the ball from the boy's hand and plunked him hard in the shoulder with it.

"Run!" Felix cried.

The lot became a battlefield as both teams went back and forth, tagging each other and dashing for home to see who would earn the right to bat next. Felix had just ducked out of the way of a ball aimed for his head when someone grabbed him by the ear and stood him up.

"Felix Schneider!" his uncle Albert yelled.

The game of tag ground to an abrupt halt and the boys shirked away as Felix's uncle laid into him.

"I knew you would be here, you worthless boy! You should have been back an hour ago! Where is the parcel you were sent to deliver?"

Felix glanced meekly at second base.

"You've buried it in the mud!?" Felix's uncle cuffed him. "If you've ruined those pieces, it'll mean both our jobs! My family will be out on the streets, and you will never earn passage for yours. Is this why you stowed away aboard that ship? To come to America and play games?"

"N-no sir."

Uncle Albert dragged Felix over to the parcel.

"Pick it up. Pick it up!"

"I didn't step on it, see? I missed the bag—"

His uncle struck him again, and Felix said nothing more. With his speed he knew he still had plenty of time to deliver the fabric pieces, and time enough to go to the Neumans', pick up their finished suits, and get them to Lord & Taylor by the close of business too. He also knew his uncle wouldn't want to hear it.

"Now go. Go!" Uncle Albert told him. "If you were my son, I'd whip you!"

And if I were your son, thought Felix as he dashed off with the parcel, *I'd run away to California.*

Felix ran to where the Neumans lived on East Eighth Street off Avenue B, in the heart of "Kleindeutschland," Little Germany. Their tenement stood in the shadow of a fancier building facing the street on the same lot. The Neumans lived on the fourth floor, two brothers and their families squeezed into a one-family flat with three rooms and no windows. Felix hated visiting there. It made him think of those preachers who stood on street corners throughout Kleindeutschland yelling warnings of damnation and hell. As much as he disliked his uncle, Felix knew that but for Uncle Albert's job as a cutter, their own Kleindeutschland flat would look like this. Or worse.

One of the Neuman boys, not much older than Felix, met him at the door. Felix only knew him from deliveries and pickups—he'd never seen any of the Neuman boys playing on Little Germany's streets or empty lots.

"Guten tag," the boy said.

"Good morning," said Felix. He held out the parcel. "I've got your new pieces."

The boy let Felix into the room. It was hot and dark, and Neumans young and old sweated as they sewed cut pieces of cloth into suits around the dim light of four flickering candles. Herr Neuman, the family "foreman," came forward to take the package from Felix.

"Danke schön," Herr Neuman said.

"You're welcome," Felix said. *"Bitte."*

Herr Neuman set the parcel on a table and opened it, counting out the pieces. He nodded to let Felix know everything was in order.

"Do you have anything for me to take back?" Felix asked. *"Haben Sie noch etwas fertig?"*

Herr Neuman held up a finger and went into another room. Felix waved to one or two of the women who looked up at him with weak smiles. Felix knew this wasn't what they had expected when they'd come to America. It wasn't what any of them had expected. Felix's own father had talked of New York as a promised land, where everyone had good jobs and plenty to eat. "Manhattan is a city of three hundred thousand," he'd said, "and half of those are men who will need a good pair of shoes." Herr Neuman, a skilled tailor, had probably said the same thing to his family about the men in Manhattan needing suits.

What neither of them knew, of course, what none of the

tailors and cobblers and haberdashers had known, was that those hundred and fifty thousand men needed only five men to sell them suits and shoes: Mr. A. T. Stewart, Messrs. Lord and Taylor, and the brothers Brooks. The five of them owned the three largest clothing stores in New York, massive, three- and four-story buildings Felix had gotten lost in more than once. Each had separate departments for men, women, and children, an army of clerks and fitters, and tables and tables of clothes, each outfit made not by a single tailor but by teams of men and women paid a fraction of what the suit cost. Felix, his uncle Albert, the Neumans, they were all just cogs in the great department store machine. Uncle Albert did nothing now but cut cloth all day, but he was better off than the Neumans, who sewed collars by candlelight sixteen hours a day, seven days a week. If they worked quickly, the Neumans might make twenty dollars a week sewing suits. Uncle Albert earned that by himself as a cutter.

Herr Neuman returned with a package of finished suits tied up with a string, and Felix left quickly, telling them he had to hurry the parcel back to Lord & Taylor but really just wanting to get away from there.

Felix ran past Tompkins Square Park to the Bowery, leaving Kleindeutschland and its crowded tenements and beer halls in his wake, but when he hit Broadway he slowed. This was Felix's favorite part of the city. Here the pigs being driven to market strutted down the sidewalk alongside flashy American women wearing their big, brightly colored dresses and ribbons. Gentlemen in serious gray suits hurried by with pocket watches in hand while b'hoys with curled mustaches and red shirts and black silk ties mocked them from painters' scaffolding and butcher shop doorways. Newsboys and street preachers shouted over each other on the corners. Buildings were torn down and rebuilt faster than Felix could keep up with them, and shootouts sometimes erupted in the streets. This wasn't the New York of the Germans or the Irish or the English, it was the New York of *Americans*, and Felix tucked his package under his arm and fell into step with the bustle of the young city.

Uncle Albert had warned him not to dawdle on the way, so he hurried along—fully intending to do his dawdling on the way back. At Lord & Taylor Felix delivered his package and picked up another, then made his way farther north on Broadway, adopting the American swagger of the lords, ladies, and swine. Felix found it easy to lose himself in Broadway's foot traffic, to be swept up by the rush and hurry of Manhattan, to hear the clatter of iron horseshoes on cobblestones and the catcalls and insults of the city's famously rude cabbies like a lullaby. On Broadway Felix was not a poor German Jew from Bremen walking the streets of a strange metropolis. Here, he was a *New Yorker*.

Felix made his way up Broadway to Madison Square, then down East Twenty-seventh Street to the corner of Fourth Avenue, where the New York Knickerbockers played baseball. He had found them by accident one day, following an oddly dressed man wearing blue woolen pantaloons, a white flannel shirt, and a straw hat, and now he went by the lot every time he ventured this far north in case a game was under way.

Felix had been overjoyed to discover grown men playing at the same game he and his friends played—only it wasn't *exactly* the same game. The Knickerbockers played three-out, all-out, but with more gentlemanly rules. For one thing, they didn't chase each other in between innings to see which team would bat next. For another, they didn't "soak" runners, but instead tried to deliver the ball to the next base before the runner could advance.

A game was under way when Felix arrived, and he joined three other spectators on a bank nearby, using the parcel with the cut cloth pieces as a seat cushion. The Striker at bat called for his pitch and smacked it to the outer field, where it was caught on the bounce.

"Hand out!" the Feeder cried, and the Striker tipped his cap and jogged merrily back to the sidelines.

Felix would have given all the sauerkraut in Klein-deutschland to be out there on the field with them. A new Striker took his place, and Felix imagined himself standing there in the blue and white uniform of the Knickerbockers, ready to deliver a base hit for his team.

The Striker bounced the first feed wide of first base, but didn't run.

"Foul ball," the Feeder called, and the Striker returned home to bat again.

This is new, Felix thought, and he watched as the Feeder pitched again and again until the Striker was able to hit the ball in the field between first and third base. Letting "foul balls" go would certainly save a lot of chasing, Felix realized, and let the fielding team concentrate its defenders in front of the batter, instead of all around him. There was still a catcher, he noted, but mainly to receive the pitches the Striker chose not to hit.

This was less and less the three-out, all-out Felix knew, but he liked it.

The next Striker put a well-placed ball in between two of the outlying fielders and scampered toward second. The ball was thrown back in quickly, and appeared to reach second base at the same time as the runner. Neither team could tell whether the Striker was out or not, and the top-hatted judge at the table beyond third base admitted he hadn't a clue. The judge came forward to examine the evidence, then threw his hands up in exasperation.

"Let us ask the young squire with the very nice shoes," one of the Knickerbockers said. With a start, Felix realized the player was talking about him. The judge and three of the players came over to where he sat.

"I—I think the ball beat the Striker," Felix told them.

"There we have it then," said the Feeder.

"Agreed," said the man in the top hat. "Umpire's decision: hand out."

"Three-out, all-out," the Feeder said, smiling. The Striker tipped his cap and jogged out onto the field to take his position at a base, but the Feeder remained on the sidelines and extended his hand. Felix shook it.

"Alexander Cartwright," the Feeder said. "And on behalf of the New York Knickerbocker Volunteer Fire Fighting Brigade, I'd like to thank you for your honest and impartial observation. I've seen you here before, haven't I?"

Felix didn't answer. He was transfixed by something over Cartwright's shoulder, a towering plume of smoke billowing up from the rooftops of the city to the south of them.

Manhattan was on fire.

2

Church bells pealed across the city, and Cartwright and the rest of the volunteer fire brigade abandoned their game and raced the few blocks to their station to ready their wagon. Felix followed behind, watching the smoke thicken. The smell of it was already heavy in the air, the way Aunt Jenell's stove smelled when first lit each morning. At the firehouse the ballplayers were quickly joined by other men who stripped off their suit coats and collars and ties and changed into the colorful blue jerseys of the Knickerbocker Volunteer Fire Fighting Brigade before taking their places around the engine. The brigade had no horse, so the cart would have to be guided by hand.

"I'm fast," Felix told Cartwright. "I can help you push."

Cartwright considered Felix's offer, and looked like he might say no. In the distance, a bigger, deeper bell started to sound over the church bells.

"If they're ringing the bell at City Hall, it's a big one. You're probably safer with us than without," Cartwright said. He tossed a blue shirt to Felix. "Put this on so we'll know you're a Knickerbocker."

Felix worked himself into the oversized shirt and grabbed hold of the wagon.

"All together now, lads," Cartwright called. "And, *push!*"

The cobblestones made the going rough at first, but as Felix and the others built up speed he felt the wagon bounce along without too much trouble. Turning was difficult, though, and as they ran the men debated the straightest path through the city.

"Fourth Avenue to Union, then Broadway south!"

"No, Broadway will be jammed! The Bowery."

Felix pushed with all his strength, but the cart had to stop as often as it started. Everywhere men and ladies poured into the street to see the smoke, making the already clogged avenue even worse. Cartwright rang the bell on the wagon and they nudged on, sending curious gawkers scurrying for the sidewalk.

And then they hit Union Square. The traffic was at a dead standstill.

"Make way! Make way! Emergency!" one of the firemen called.

But no one could move. The streets were so hopelessly packed it was almost impossible to cross the square on foot. Horses reared in the close quarters. Carriages scraped the sides of cabs and omnibuses. Men yelled obscenities at each other. Across the square a fistfight broke out. Cartwright gave the bell an angry clang and slapped his hat on the tank. Through the tree-lined hills of Union Square, Felix could see their destination—the open expanse of Fourth Avenue south of the Bowery.

"Mr. Cartwright," Felix called. "The park!"

At first Cartwright didn't understand, but then he nodded and smiled at Felix and went to work again on his bell.

"Let us through! Make way! Push on to the park, lads!"

It took them a full quarter of an hour to ford the frozen river of carriages the short distance to the corner of Union Square Park, upsetting an apple cart and managing to turn another carriage completely around on the way. Felix wondered if they'd just made things worse, but it was the fire, not the traffic, that mattered now. The closer they got, the more Felix worried the fire was in Kleindeutschland. The entire skyline to the south was grayish black.

At last the Knickerbockers pushed their engine up the curb into the wooded expanse of the park. One or two of the stranded drivers close by cursed them, but Felix thought they were probably just sore at not having thought of it first. With a heave, the volunteer firefighters started their shortcut across the square. A couple of the men near Felix gave him smiles and patted him on the back.

The smiles soon turned to scowls, however, as none of them had ever reckoned how difficult it was to run up a park hill with a cast-iron tank. Felix dug in with his good shoes and gave it all he was worth, and with great effort the brigade slogged its way up and down the rolling hills of the park. An explosion to the south—a gas line, one of the men guessed—brought screams from the ladies caught in the throng of carriages around the square. Felix redoubled his efforts. There was another sea of vehicles to cross when they reached the other side of the square, but like a needle through leather they eventually found their way through, and the angry glares from the volunteers became smiles and weary pats on the back again.

South of Union Square Felix and the Knickerbockers were back at a trot, the streets clear of everyone now but rescue workers. Everyone else had fled farther north.

"The size of that smoke cloud, three or four buildings must be on fire," one of the company guessed. "Perhaps a whole city block."

The sky was black as coal as they drew near, and to Felix's relief it wasn't Kleindeutschland that was on fire. It wasn't three or four buildings that were burning, though. It wasn't even three or four blocks. *All of lower Manhattan* was on fire. Local fire brigades were already on the scene, and more poured in from all over the city: First two, then five, then nine, then fourteen, and more, but Felix began to despair that there would never be enough. Buildings burned down Water Street as far as Felix could see.

The heat from the flames was blistering as the Knickerbockers searched for an unoccupied cistern to drop their hose in. The air itself wobbled, as though the fire was melting it. Against the overpowering heat was the strange sensation that it was snowing, and Felix watched as burned-out cinders the size of quarters fell on everything, turning the Knickerbockers' bright blue uniforms to the color of thick gray ash. He could taste it too; it was like he had licked a stovepipe. The heat and the ash made Felix's eyes water, but his tears evaporated almost as quickly as they came.

The Knickerbockers pulled to a stop as the blaze rose from the roof of a five-story building beside them. The wind off the East River carried the fire like swirling leaves across the street, where it set the canvas awnings of another building ablaze. Suddenly the fire brigade was not on the edge of the inferno, but inside it.

Felix spun. Fire was everywhere around him and he panicked. His family seemed very far away from him now, more than a passenger ticket away, more than an ocean away. He felt sealed off from his family back in Bremen by a wall of flame, and for the first time in his life he thought he might die before seeing his mother and father again.

A hand on his shoulder stopped his spinning.

"Keep your head," Cartwright told him. "I never meant you to come this far, lad, but I'll see you safely home."

The Knickerbockers pushed on to William Street to escape the blaze, but the air there was too thick to breathe. One of the men collapsed, choking and gasping, and Felix helped haul him up onto the cart before they retreated to Hanover Street, where one of the company knew a cistern could be found. No brigade had yet laid claim to it, and the Knickerbockers pried off the lid to the underground reservoir and snaked down their hose. Two of the brawniest members of the brigade took to the hand pump, and soon water was gushing through the network of hoses Felix helped put together. Water splashed from the nozzle into the broken windows of a clerical office, but after half an hour it was obvious to Felix that they weren't doing any good. If anything, the fire was getting worse.

From the look on Cartwright's face, he thought the same thing.

"The fire's too strong," he yelled over the clang of the bells, the rush of the water, and the roar of the flames.

"What can we do?" Felix asked. His skin was coated with a thick film of sweat, and his tongue tasted like burned matches.

"Maybe farther back—Wall Street, or Pine—"

Glass shattered and rained down on the sidewalk as the fire ate its way down through the floors of the warehouse behind them.

"The dry goods!" Cartwright yelled. "Salvage what you can before the buildings collapse!"

Men traded out places at the hand pumps to keep the water coming while the rest of the brigade smashed their way into warehouses with axes and hooks. Felix stood back, waiting until the doors were knocked down and the entrances sprayed with water to rush inside with the others. The first storehouse

Felix entered was filled with bolts of cloth—suit material like the kind he ran back and forth to Lord & Taylor. He and Cartwright began heaping the stuff in the middle of the street. Rolls of cottons, woolens, and silks joined bags of coffee beans, mounds of lace, stacks of paper records, bottles of liquor—anything and everything that could be saved.

Conditions grew worse and worse. One team barely escaped a vicious backdraft. Another became trapped when a second story fell in, and the men had to be rescued with axes.

"That's it, young squire," Cartwright told Felix. "You're confined to the wagon."

A man in a fire chief's hat rode up on a horse before Felix could argue.

"The fire's out of control, Mr. Anderson," Cartwright said. "We're doing all we can to save the goods in these warehouses, but—"

Felix saw the fiery piece of debris fluttering down toward the pile of stores in the street before anyone else, but there was nothing he could do—nothing any of them could have done. The moment it touched down the lace caught fire, then the cotton, and almost at once the mountain of dry goods was a blazing bonfire that drove them off the street.

"Fall back!" the fire chief called. "Retreat!"

The fire truck was trapped on the other side of the pyre, but the pumpers ran it through, singeing themselves and the cart in the process. Cartwright and the others turned what was left in the tank on the boys who'd come through the flames to make sure they were extinguished, and then everyone fell back to Wall Street.

"The glow and the smoke are so strong that crews from Philadelphia and New Haven turned out in their own suburbs, thinking the blaze was in their own cities," the fire chief said, his horse dancing backward, the only one among them with the sense to run. "The Pennsylvania and Connecticut crews telegraphed to say they're on the way, but they'll not be here in time to prevent the conflagration from jumping Wall Street."

Felix knew what that meant. Lower Manhattan was all businesses and warehouses, but beyond the road where a real wall had once stood were residences. Apartments. People. The thirty thousand souls who called the island their home. If the fire blew north, it could overtake City Hall and the Five Points slums. If it blew to the northeast, it might spread as far as the crowded tenements of Kleindeutschland—Felix's home.

"Powder then?" Cartwright asked.

The fire chief nodded. "Some of the boys are already rowing across to the Navy Yard in Brooklyn, but they may not be in time."

"We'll round up what we can from the groceries," said Cartwright.

"Godspeed," Mr. Anderson told them, and he rode off to find the next brigade.

"We need powder, and lots of it, lads!" Cartwright announced to the Knickerbockers. "Take it from wherever you can, and meet back here!"

Felix ran with Cartwright, ignoring the command to stay with the wagon.

"Powder, sir?"

"Gunpowder. We'll blow up the buildings that have not yet caught fire and deprive the inferno of its fuel."

The idea sounded crazy to Felix. Fight fire with gunpowder?

They found a grocery on Pine Street and another on Nassau where they collected small amounts of gunpowder. What he knew to be only a few minutes' run felt like a lifetime to Felix, the heat and howl of the fire at their heels like some kind of wild animal. Soon though they rejoined the other Knickerbockers, and the buildings up and down the block were divided up by team. Cartwright took their small barrel of gunpowder and Felix followed close behind.

"We'll want to place it near a supporting column," he told Felix. "We need to bring the whole building down before the fire reaches it."

Felix held the cask while Cartwright broke down the door with an axe. Inside it was dark and cluttered, with crates and boxes stacked on the floor and behind counters.

"Can we at least empty the stores first?" Felix asked.

"No time," Cartwright said. "If any of these buildings catches fire before they all go up, none of this will do any good. There—there's a post near the back. We'll put the gunpowder against that and—"

And Cartwright was gone, dropping from Felix's sight with a cry and a cracking thud. Felix felt a foot step off into nothing, then caught his balance and stumbled back before he fell. As his eyes adjusted, he saw the large black hole in the floor.

"Mr. Cartwright!" he called. "Mr. Cartwright, are you all right?"

There was a soft moan from below, then a match struck, illuminating Cartwright's pained face.

"Basement storage," he grunted. With the light, Felix could see ropes dangling on pulleys. The hole was built to haul crates up from the hold below.

"Do you—do you need me to pull you up?" he asked.

Cartwright shook his head, wincing. "There's a staircase. Near the back. But I think I've broken my ankle."

Felix worked his way to the rear of the building, sliding one foot in front of him the whole way to avoid any more pitfalls. He set the cask of gunpowder by the support beam and found the stairs, taking them two at a time. Cartwright waited for him at the bottom. Felix helped him to his feet and supported him as they climbed back upstairs.

"We'll have to send someone else in to light the charge," Cartwright told him. "I'll never be fast enough like this."

Explosions thundered nearby as Felix helped Cartwright hobble outside. Clouds of wood and dust blasted from the collapsing structures, shattering the windows and shredding the awnings of the buildings on the other side of the street. One by one the warehouses came toppling down into heaps, the fire behind them flinching back from the detonations.

Felix dragged Cartwright into the lee of an alleyway across the street, and together they watched as bright sparks landed on the roof of the building they'd just escaped.

"Hurry—tell the men—"

Felix plucked the box of matches from Cartwright's vest pocket. "No time!" he called, already running back toward the building. Cartwright yelled for him to stop, but Felix knew that by the time they could find someone else to run inside and light the charge it would be too late. The line had to be drawn here, now, and like Cartwright said, if one building survived, the fire would push through.

Felix dashed inside, slowing around the hole in the floor and then running to where the small powder keg sat on the floor. It wasn't enough to let the fire outside reach the explosive and blow it up—by then the flames would have spread from rooftop to rooftop and crossed Wall Street to the businesses and homes on the other side. It had to be done now, and it had to be done quickly.

Felix eyed the long fuse on the keg, then bent it double so it would ignite twice as fast when he lit it.

"I am the fastest boy in Manhattan," Felix whispered. "I am the fastest boy in all of New York." He struck a match and readied himself like he was a runner on first base. "I am the fastest boy in America."

Felix lit the fuse and ran. He ran harder and faster than he had ever run in his life. The fuse hissed furiously behind him. Felix made the turn around the hole in the floor like he was rounding third base and he sprinted for the dim light of the front door like it was home. He was almost there, almost there, almost—

The blast lifted Felix off his feet and threw him into a headfirst slide over the sidewalk. *Ace!* Felix thought, and then he hit the ground and his world went black.

3

Felix awoke in a strange room and a strange bed. A dim light came in through the lone window in the wall and Felix blinked, trying to focus his eyes. The first thing he saw was Uncle Albert's face.

"Worthless boy," Uncle Albert said. He smiled softly.

"Worthless? This boy? He very likely saved the city." Felix turned. Alexander Cartwright sat on the other side of his bed, holding a cane.

"Do not overstate the matter," Uncle Albert said.

"Where—?" Felix tried.

"The Brooklyn City Hospital," Cartwright said. "Or what will be."

Felix saw now that there were three other beds in the small room, all with patients in them. He tried to sit up, but pain in his stomach and legs pushed him down again.

"Don't stir," Uncle Albert said. "You're still unwell."

"The explosion caught you as you ran through the door. It threw you all the way across the street. Do you remember?"

Felix closed his eyes. He remembered flying through the air—scoring an ace.

"The building?" Felix asked.

"It came down in time," Cartwright said. "The fire was contained, but it's been burning for days."

"Days?"

"You've been unconscious for some time," Uncle Albert said. "Your aunt Jenell has been very worried about you."

"Though she hasn't been the one at your side day and night," Cartwright said. Uncle Albert blushed, something Felix had never seen before, and he stood with his hat in his hand.

"My legs feel strange," Felix said. "Cold."

Uncle Albert put a blanket on Felix's legs. "I—I must go and tell Jenell," he said. "She will want to know you are awake." Uncle Albert put a hand to Felix's shoulder, then left quickly. Cartwright stood with the help of his cane and went over to the window.

"It's still smoldering, you know. They say the smoke plume can be seen two hundred miles away. It's all gone now. The last of what was New Amsterdam lays in ruins."

"New Amsterdam?"

"What they once called New York, when it was a Dutch settlement. Didn't you know? That's where we got our name—the Knickerbockers. That's the word people use for the Dutch settlers and their descendants. It's from that Irving novel, I think."

Felix had no idea what novel Cartwright was talking about, but it didn't matter.

"I wonder how many Knickerbockers there really are left in New York," Cartwright said. "Everything's changing so fast. I imagine everything that burned down will be replaced within a year. Newer, bigger, better."

"Your leg, sir," Felix said. "Is it greatly injured?"

"What, this?" Cartwright said. "A sprain. I'll be running the bases again in no time." Cartwright caught himself, as though he had said something he hadn't meant to, and turned again to the window.

"Your uncle tells me you stowed away to come here, young squire. That you ran away from home. I wonder, were you running *to* America, or away from something there?"

"Both, I suppose," Felix said. "Things were so bad in Bremen. No work, no food. And everyone said there was both in America, that a man could make his fortune here, no matter where he came from or what he started with. My father had no money to come, so I ran away and hid on a ship. I came here to work and make money and earn enough to bring my family over so we could be happy again."

"Do you regret it, coming here?"

"Oh no! I miss my family, but I've almost saved enough to bring them to America, and then I can show them Broadway and the fine ladies in their dresses and the pigs and the five-story department stores—and baseball!"

Cartwright laughed. "I think maybe baseball *is* America.

The spirit of it, at least. Something we brought with us from the Old World and made our own, the way we made this country." He turned from the window. "I'm getting ready to run away myself, I think. West, to California. They say the hills are full of gold."

Uncle Albert came back in then, bringing Aunt Jenell with him. She smothered Felix in her embrace.

"I think I'll turn you over to your aunt and uncle," Cartwright said, but Uncle Albert and Aunt Jenell wouldn't let him leave without pumping his hand and thanking him again and again. Aunt Jenell even surprised Cartwright with a hug.

"Good-bye, young squire," Cartwright said. He shook Felix's hand. "I hope this doesn't slow down your dreams."

"What does he mean, this slowing down my dreams?" Felix asked when Cartwright was gone.

"Mr. Cartwright was so kind," Aunt Jenell said. "He paid for all your hospital care. We couldn't have afforded it otherwise."

"But Felix, my boy," Uncle Albert said, "we've had to spend the money you saved to bring your family to America. I'm sorry. The fire, it has put so many people out of work, including me. When the warehouses burned, there was less cloth to be cut, and with less cloth to be cut, they do not need so many cutters. I've been let go."

"All the money I've saved? But—" Felix didn't understand, wanted to demand how they could just use up the money he'd put aside, but the way his aunt and uncle stared at the floor in shame told him they must have had no choice. "But . . . there will be work again, won't there?" Felix asked. "Cartwright said everything will be rebuilt."

"But not soon enough for us," Uncle Albert said. "We had very little savings. You know that. We—we've had to move from our apartment in Kleindeutschland."

"Albert has found us work here in Brooklyn. Sewing suits."

No, Felix thought—not that. Not living in the darkness, working his fingers to the bone for pennies like the Neumans.

"But my job as a runner—I can still do that. If there are pieces to be sewn, there must be someone running them to the department stores!"

Albert and Jenell shared a sad look, and his aunt put a hand on Felix's leg.

"Felix, your legs—they were injured in the explosion."

What? No—it couldn't be. But the strange cold sensation he had . . . Felix ripped the sheets and blankets off. Underneath, his legs were blackened and scarred.

"They've given you a drug, to combat the pain," Uncle Albert told him. "They say the pain will get better, but that it will never go away."

Felix didn't want to cry, but the tears came whether he wanted them or not. He was the fastest boy in New York. The fastest boy in *America.* His legs had taken him across

Germany and across an ocean to a new world. It was on his legs that he had planned to carry his mother and father and baby sister away from the blight and the famine and the poverty of Bremen. It was on his legs that his family's future depended, and now here they lay, ashen and crippled like Lower Manhattan itself.

Aunt Jenell wrapped him in another hug and let him cry.

✛ ✛ ✛

Uncle Albert carried Felix home from the hospital the next day, even though Felix could walk passably well. What he couldn't do was run, and Felix wondered what the point of having feet at all was if he couldn't do that. His shoes too, the beautiful shoes his father had made for him, his only connection to the family he'd left behind, had been so mangled and burned in the explosion that they were unusable now. Felix didn't want to see them, had told his uncle to throw them away, but Uncle Albert had insisted on keeping them. The leather, he said, could be used for something else.

On the way to their new flat Felix saw a group of boys playing three-out, all-out in a pig field. They were in between innings, chasing each other around with the ball to see who would bat next, ignoring the pigs the way the uptown ladies and gentlemen did on Broadway.

Felix turned his head away so he couldn't see, and told his uncle to keep walking.

Their new apartment was much like the Neumans', only

they shared it not with more Schneiders but with another family, the Smiths. They had been Schmidts, but changed their name to something more American in the hopes of landing better work. Uncle Albert was considering doing the same.

There were two bedrooms in the Schneider/Smith home— one for each of the families—and a small kitchen where they all shared meals and sewing work. Felix's new job was stitching the broad, flat pieces of suit jackets together while Aunt Jenell pieced the sleeves. Uncle Albert, a master tailor, did the more complicated parts. Like the Neumans, they had no windows in their flat, and in the summer the heat was stifling. By midday Felix was so sweaty the needle would slip right out of his hand.

When the runner came to pick up their work, Felix would disappear into one of the bedrooms.

Life went on this way for more weeks and months than Felix could count. Uncle Albert didn't change their last name, but he did join a Christian church, which gave them Sundays off. Sometimes Felix would take his free day and wander down to the docks at the end of Flatbush Avenue and watch the city across the East River recover in stages. First one warehouse, then another, then a tall office building, a bank, a dry-goods store. Like Cartwright said, always newer, bigger, better.

Felix saw too the huge masted steamers with flywheels amidships, like the one he had stolen away on to cross the

Atlantic, unloading thousands of new immigrants upon the docks at the Battery as they had once delivered him. Felix remembered his first steps into this crowded new world of hope and promise, and he longed to be one of them again, a greenhorn fresh off the boat, ready to make his fortune and bring his family to the New World. There on the Brooklyn pier, Felix resolved to start again.

That night while everyone else slept, Felix found a wine cork in the kitchen and wrapped yards of twine and thread around it. When that was done he pulled out the pair of shoes his father had made for him, and with Uncle Albert's shears he cut away the charred leather and trimmed what was left into wide strips. Then, using a thick needle and the laces from his useless shoes, he began to sew the leather strips around the outside of his twine ball. When he was finished, Felix scratched a small *S* on his new baseball, an *S* for Schneider.

Cartwright had said that baseball *was* America, and somehow, some way, Felix would find a way to get back in the game. Even if it took him a lifetime to do it. Even if it took him *nine* lifetimes to do it. Felix would play ball again.

Second Inning: The Red-Legged Devil

Northern Virginia, 1864

1

"I reckon that's the best baseball in Spotsylvania, Virginia," Stuart said.

"I reckon this is the *only* baseball in Spotsylvania, Virginia," Louis Schneider said. He flipped his father's baseball high in the air and dashed forward to catch it.

"Louis! Will you stop!? We could be set upon by Rebs any second!"

Stuart's skittishness was understandable, if a little tiresome. Louis had been there for Stuart's rookie engagement in the Civil War—what the career men called "Seeing the Elephant"—and had seen Stuart come away the worse for it. After their first battle, most men went one way or the other: They either got crazy, or they got scared. Stuart got scared. He'd been a jumble of nerves ever since, and the whole time they'd been on patrol today he'd jumped and twitched at every little sound.

Louis sighed and stowed the baseball away in his

haversack, extracting a copy of *Beadle's Dime Baseball Player* to look at as the two walked their patrol.

"Where on Earth'd you find that?"

"My pa sent it to me. He's a top rail player, only he could never go pro because of his legs. Got messed up in an explosion."

"In—in the war?" Stuart asked.

"No, fighting a fire when he was a kid. That's why I joined the Army—because he couldn't."

Stuart peered at Louis. "Just how old *are* you, anyway?"

"Sixteen," Louis lied. "Say, it says here the National Association voted the fly rule in. No more catching a ball on the bounce."

"Uh-huh."

"What? I'm serious," Louis said, but he knew Stuart was still on about his age.

Stuart stopped and tensed, gripping his rifle in both hands. Louis looked ahead and saw a little general store at a crossroads. A thin trail of smoke rose from the chimney pipe.

"Say, you don't suppose it's *open*, do you?" Louis asked.

"You're not thinking of going in there! Louis, we're deep into Virginia. What if the owner is a Confederate?"

Louis grinned. "I'm counting on it. Follow my lead."

Louis bounded up the steps into the store but froze inside the door. To his amazement, it was stocked like a Brooklyn Heights grocers. There were barrels of fresh apples, carrots, and pecans, hunks of salt pork, sacks of flour and cornmeal and potatoes, shelves of fresh bread, rows of eggs. For a moment, he and Stuart stood in the doorway drooling. It was all Louis could do to keep from lunging for the first scrumptious morsel in sight and not cease eating until he was arrested or shot, whichever came first.

The shopkeeper came out from a small pantry in the back and stopped short when he saw them. Louis and Stuart weren't wearing Union blues, but they weren't wearing Confederate grays either. The shopkeeper's hand disappeared beneath the counter and came back with a pistol, which he laid down beside the register.

"I'll have no trouble now, you hear?" he told the boys.

Louis stepped forward with his hands in the air. "And we don't aim to cause any."

The shopkeeper nodded at them. "What kind of costume is that, anyway? French? Hessian?"

"We're the Brooklyn Fourteenth," Louis told him. "We're with the Army of the Potomac."

Beside him, Louis could hear Stuart hiss. The grocer picked up his gun again.

"This ain't a commissary, neither Union nor otherwise. You either got money or you don't—and I charge double for Yankees."

That told Louis all he needed to know. Heedless of the shopkeeper's gun, he strolled through the aisles, surveying the goods like he was shopping.

"Louis, let's get out of here," Stuart whispered for all to hear.

Louis ignored him and spoke to the grocer. "Oh, I've got a bit of money," he said. "But I'm afraid it's just this worthless Confederate stuff." He pulled a few small bills out of his pocket and set them on the counter. "I understand it's not good for much of anything. Like everything else down here."

The shopkeeper raised himself up, insulted.

"So long as the Confederacy still stands, boy, those notes will be good in my store."

"Is that so?" Louis asked. He took off his haversack and withdrew two handfuls of bills—almost five hundred dollars in Confederate money—and put them on the counter.

"In that case," Louis told him, "we'll take everything you've got."

✢ ✢ ✢

They didn't really buy everything, of course—just as much as they could carry. But that was plenty enough for a first-rate feast, and when they returned, Louis and Stuart were hailed by their fellow soldiers as heroes to the nation.

"It was all Louis," Stuart told them, regaling the rest of the Brooklyn Fourteenth with the story as he lazed by the fire, licking the chicken grease off his fingers.

"Lucky Louis!" one of the boys said with a laugh.

"Lucky nothing—where'd you come by so many Confederate bills?" asked Corporal Bruner.

"Well, I'll tell you," Louis said. "Every night after a fight,

I wait 'til late and sneak back onto the field of battle and go through the Rebs' coats."

"You can't be serious!"

"Why not? They do it to themselves so's there's hardly a thing left anyway—except all that no-account cash. I was just collecting it to take home as souvenirs. I never figured on buying anything with it. Never thought I'd have the chance."

"Lucky Louis," somebody said again.

Not lucky enough to earn a promotion, thought Louis, although he'd certainly put in his time. He'd lied about his age three years ago so he could march to Washington in '61 with the Fourteenth and beg to go to war. They let him march, but perhaps suspecting he was underage they only made him a drummer. Louis had taken over as standard bearer when Johnson took a bullet to the head at Antietam, and then had a rifle thrust in his hands at Fredericksburg. He'd battled the graybacks at Chancellorsville, spent three days dodging bullets at Gettysburg, fought in the Battle of the Wilderness, and been in half again as many skirmishes in between. Maybe he was lucky after all. Of the eleven hundred boys and men who'd left Brooklyn to the cheers of their city, only one hundred and forty-three remained. The rest, like Stuart, were fresh fish from home.

Louis took out the baseball again and flipped it between his hands. He wasn't lucky, he thought. It was the ball. His father had given it to him the day he left for the war, telling

41

him to bring it back in one piece. Louis figured his father wouldn't have let that ball go without knowing he'd get it back, which meant as long as he had it, he couldn't help but come home safe and sound. He ran a thumb over the *S* scratched in the leather, the *S* for Schneider.

A sergeant who'd been with them from the first clapped a hand on Louis's shoulder.

"Have a game with that ball of yours?" he asked.

"Could do," Louis told him. "If I can ever get up off this spot again."

The sergeant laughed. "Let us know. There's a lad from the Tenth Massachusetts who's challenged us to a match."

"I'm happy to beat the bean eaters any old time they wish," Louis told him. "But only if they'll play by New York rules. I'd rather the game not last three days."

Soldiers suddenly began scrambling for their caps and coats. Stuart leaped to his feet and knocked over the kettle before falling to the ground himself.

"What is it?" he asked. "Are we under attack?"

Louis stood. "General coming!" a sergeant yelled, running through the camp. "Make ready to present! General coming!"

Louis buttoned up his uniform and helped Stuart to his feet. They scurried to attention under the watchful eye of Lieutenant Tinker as a horse's hoofbeats drew closer.

"Atten-*tion!*" Tinker cried, and the Fourteenth stood straight.

The man who rode up was known to Louis and the others

who had been with the regiment the longest: He was General Abner Doubleday, the man who had commanded the Brooklyn Fourteenth at Antietam and again at Gettysburg. He was a stout man, as most generals were, with a hulking brown mustache, long tall nose, and receding line of dark curly hair. Louis counted him brave if not brilliant for his actions on the battlefield, though none of the boys thought the worse of him.

Doubleday pulled his mount to a stop before them and surveyed their lines.

"The Brooklyn Fourteenth," he said. "The Red-Legged Devils."

They had gotten the nickname after Bull Run, where it was said they had fought with hell's fury. General McDowell even let them keep their red breeches and hats as badges of honor when the rest of the army was issued standard blues. The Fourteenth's uniforms, like their boys, were supplied by the City of Brooklyn herself.

Doubleday rode up and down the lines inspecting them, then stopped to speak.

"On many a weary march, and many a hard fought field, I have personally seen your courage and devotion. Your name is a household word in the army. You are the elite of our division."

Louis stood a little straighter.

"You original members who mustered in during the formation of your regiment—you who have survived Bull

Run, South Mountain, Falmouth, Antietam, Fredericksburg, Rappahanock Station, Chancellorsville, Sulphur Springs, Gettysburg, Groveton, The Wilderness, Gainesville, and Spotsylvania Court House—*twice*—you brave few who remain have earned your nation's respect and gratitude. You have also earned your release from the Army of the Potomac."

Lucky again! Louis looked at those in Company K who had been around from the beginning. One or two of them were crying, but whether they were tears of joy or sorrow Louis didn't know. For his part, it was as though a great weight had lifted off his shoulders. His father's baseball had seen him through.

"Tomorrow morning you will take a train to Baltimore, and thence to Jersey City and home to Brooklyn, where your city fathers are even now, I am told, making ready a celebration of some consequence." The general sniffed the air and moved his horse closer to one of the campfires. "Although I gather you've already had something of a celebration here today."

A ripple of laughter rode through the company.

"I do swear, I have never known a regiment so full of shrewd devices to avoid unnecessary hardships as the Brooklyn Fourteenth. Where in tarnation did you—no, I had better not know."

"If you'd care to have a game with us," called Corporal Rugge, "we plan to play baseball next!"

The general laughed. "I have no talent or interest for baseball," said Doubleday. "But I would very much like to sample whatever is brewing in that pot over yonder."

"Company *dis*-missed!" cried Lieutenant Tinker. The soldiers relaxed and fell out of ranks, and the general worked his way back to the homemade still, congratulating those who would be sent home.

Stuart hugged his friend. "You've made it, Louis! Lucky Louis, you're headed home for Brooklyn!"

"Perhaps I'll be home in time to see the Atlantics play the Eckfords for the championship."

"If the Putnams don't win it!"

"Have you heard? They've put up a fence around the Union grounds and are charging ten cents admission to see their games!"

Stuart shook his head. "Paying admission will be the ruin of baseball. What's next, paying the players?"

Louis smiled. For once Stuart wasn't listening for the snap of twigs and the report of rifles.

"Come on," Louis told him. "Let's go have a game. And we won't charge the trees and rocks any admission to watch."

They had more than enough to play among their own company, and the officers set to choosing up sides. The Fourteenth had a serviceable piece of oak they used for a bat, and the bases were measured off according to the New York rules. The fly rule was agreed upon, as most players thought catching the ball on the fly was more manly anyway, but "stealing" bases, a new practice introduced by Ned Cuthbert of the Philadelphia Keystones, was deemed unsportsmanlike and prohibited. General Doubleday was solicited to call balls and strikes, but he had other companies to see and so the teams made do with Lieutenant Tinker.

That day Louis heard it said that a more delightful afternoon of baseball was never had in Virginia nor, it was argued, at any time in Manhattan or Long Island. He had to agree. Corporal Bruner pitched as well as James Creighton of the Brooklyn Excelsiors, and Stuart drew applause for a fine diving catch made on a fly to the outfield.

On Louis's third time at bat there were Red-Legged Devils standing on first and second with the score tied at six aces apiece. Louis was eager to have another go at Bruner's dastardly "dew drops," the balls that seemed to float across the plate as leaves descend to the forest floor, and his mates cheered him on from the sidelines. Bruner lofted the ball and Louis waited, waited, waited—and then swung, striking the ball high in the air toward Stuart in center field. Louis watched him track back on it as he ran, then, surprisingly, Stuart broke off his pursuit of the ball and turned to stare at the edge of the woods.

"Wait, I think there's somebody—" he started to call out, but he never finished. The pop of a rifle and the telltale puff of blue-gray smoke came out of the woods, and Stuart's leg exploded. In a moment the air was full of bumblebees, whizzing lead balls that cracked into the trees and the dirt.

Louis's run toward third became a sprint for his life. The shots brought men in their long johns scurrying from the Union camp with rifles in hand, and while those playing the game looked for holes to crawl into, the rest of the Red-Legged Devils came charging into the clearing to meet the Confederates in the forest.

What started as a skirmish turned into a full-scale battle, giving Louis and the other ballplayers time enough to go back for their rifles and rejoin the fight. The Brooklyn Fourteenth drove the rebels into the forest again, and then the Confederates, receiving reinforcements, pushed the Union soldiers back to their camp. When dusk fell there was no clear winner, as was so often the case in engagements like this, and Lieutenant Tinker received orders to break camp and retreat.

Louis marched with his company two miles inland under cover of night, and they set up their tents by a small stream. The camp canard had the rest of the regiment moving on to North Anna, some two days away, while Louis and the rest who had received their release would be transported to the nearest railway station when it was safe and then ferried northward and homeward.

But Louis couldn't go back to Brooklyn. Not yet. He had, alas, lost two things on the field of battle he could not leave behind: his friend Palmer Stuart, and the best and only baseball in Spotsylvania, Virginia.

2

"You can't go back."

Louis took the powder and shot out of his haversack and weighed them, then handed them to Corporal Bruner.

"Without a rifle too? Are you crazy, Schneider?"

"Too heavy," whispered Louis. "Need to travel light."

The camp was sleeping but for the pickets who kept watch. Louis looked around, trying not to think of it as the last time he would see his friends. Those who were headed home tomorrow were probably dreaming of family and hot baths and tables full of food. He didn't have to guess what nightmares the others who were staying dreamed of.

"It's not worth it, Schneider. You go home tomorrow," Bruner told him.

"Stuart's still back there," Louis said. "He was my friend. I can't just—"

"Stuart's dead and you know it."

Louis considered that.

"He only took a ball to the leg. I saw it."

"I saw it too. He's dead."

The cool night air was sharp, and Louis could see his breath hanging in front of him like some still image caught on tintype. In it, he felt the truth of the situation laid bare.

"If he's dead, I'll find my ball and be back before light."

Louis could feel Bruner's eyes on him in the dark. "Is that what this is about? That baseball?"

"I can't go back without it," Louis told him. "It's my lucky baseball. Besides, my pa would kill me."

"You go back there and Johnny Reb'll do the killing for him. If you're lucky. Or be taken to some Confederate prison camp if you're not."

They'd all heard the tales of the Southern prison camps. Compared to that, death did seem the better alternative. Louis hefted his haversack to his shoulder just the same.

"Your family's gonna be right sore you went and got yourself killed the night before you was heading home. Especially over a baseball."

How could Louis make him understand? It was more than a baseball. Louis's pa had given it to him when he left, with the order to bring it back in one piece. But they both knew he hadn't been talking about the baseball. His pa couldn't allow that Louis might get blown to bits like Stuart, or Kurlanski, or Jones, or any of the hundreds of other boys Louis had seen get mustered out the hard way on the field of battle. In time Louis had begun to think of the ball as himself, or the ball as a part of him maybe—he hadn't really tried to make sense of it. All he knew was that one way or another, both of them would end up back in Brooklyn one day, having a game with the boys at Pigtown.

"I'll be back before light," Louis said again. He and Bruner shook hands, and Louis tromped off through the forest the way they had come earlier that day.

The picket post was more on guard tonight, but when they saw Louis they smiled.

"Ain't you got enough souvenirs already?" one of the boys on duty whispered. The regulars were used to Louis slipping away to collect money from the dead graybacks, and he usually jawed with them on the way out. Tonight Louis gave them a wave but passed by without a word.

The moon was a sliver in the dark sky, which was good and bad. Good that it would be hard for anyone to spot him; bad that it was hard for Louis to see anything himself. He found the road to Spotsylvania Court House and worked his way alongside it through the woods. Occasionally he'd come to a cleared field and have to crouch along the roadside, trying to stay low and unseen. He reached instinctively to touch the baseball in his haversack, then remembered it wasn't there. Louis got scared on the battlefield—no man he knew could say he didn't—but now he began to feel as Stuart must have, that there was always someone lurking around the next corner, behind the nearest bush, the closest tree, someone waiting to send a lead ball buzzing his way with his name on it. Poor Stuart had been right once, and once was all it took.

A dark figure appeared in the road ahead, and Louis flattened himself in a ditch, feeling the cold wet grass against his face. He wished for all his life he had his father's baseball back. Or his rifle. He cursed himself for leaving it behind.

The shape grew closer, and with his ears attuned to every little sound, Louis heard a man's boots scraping along the hard dirt path. *Thunk,* scrape. *Thunk,* scrape. Something was off about the way he was walking, and Louis dared to raise his head to take a look.

The scraping stopped.

"Who's there?" came a voice.

Louis buried his head again in the ditch and cursed silently.

"Be you grayback or bush hog, show yourself, varmint!"

Louis slowly lifted himself and stood. Better to die on his feet than facedown in a ditch—and in the dark, there was always a chance he might be able to run.

Louis squinted and tried to see the other man in the dark. He was only a shadow, but from his silhouette Louis could see he was leaning on a pole or a stick. Or a rifle.

"Friend or foe?" the man asked.

"That depends on what color uniform you're wearing," Louis said.

"Union blue," the man told him. "Army of the Potomac, First New Jersey Brigade."

"I hail from just across the river, friend. Brooklyn Fourteenth."

Louis stepped close enough so they could see each other in the dim light.

"Private First Class Louis Schneider," he said, shaking the man's hand.

"Corporal Giuseppe Silvestri."

"You coming from Spotsylvania?" Louis asked.

He nodded. "You coming from the camp? Am I close?"

"About another mile," Louis told him. He saw now the man had a leg wound, and he grimaced. It wasn't as bad as Stuart's, but the shirt he'd tied around it was already soaked with blood.

"You taking French leave, son?" He meant was Louis running away.

"No, I'm headed back to Spotsylvania to check on a friend I left behind. Is it much farther?"

"'Bout another hour or so, best I can reckon. Not much to go back for that didn't hobble away or get carried away though."

"You run into any Rebs from here to there?" Louis asked.

"No. You're the first ghost I've seen."

"Same here," Louis said. "Just keep down this road, then take the right junction at the forge. You'll come along the advance pickets, and they can get you into camp."

"Much obliged, Private."

Louis gave the man a quick salute, and they parted ways.

He stayed on guard the rest of his walk, but if the corporal hadn't seen any Confederates, ambling along at his cripple's pace, Louis figured he wasn't likely to meet the Army of Northern Virginia on the way.

In an hour or so the terrain began to look familiar and Louis picked his way off the main road into the woods where he thought they had been encamped. He caught a whiff of gun smoke on the air and he knew he was close. Soon he was upon the smoldering campfires of the day before, the roasted chicken and the baseball game distant memories now. It was late at night—or early the next day—and Louis shook his head and blinked his eyes to keep himself alert.

He started stepping over bodies before he ever reached the field. The soldiers, both Union and Confederate, lay faceup, which meant the surgeons had been here. After a battle the surgeons would roll in with their ambulances and stretchers and take some of the injured, but not all. Those that were only slightly wounded, like the corporal Louis had met on the road, were left to make their own way back to camp or to a field hospital; those with mortal wounds were left to die. In Louis's late-night skulks back to battlefields he had always made a point of waiting until well after the surgeons had finished their business.

It was brighter out in the open of the field, though still dark, and men laid out all over the field looked like they were sleeping. Louis knew better. He made his way quickly to where Stuart had been playing center field. He hoped not to find him, for that would mean the surgeons had gotten him and thought his wounds operable—but there he was, lying faceup and staring at the moon with dead eyes.

Louis closed Stuart's eyes and said a short prayer over him, then cast around for his baseball. He found it lying a few yards away in the tall grass and returned with it to Stuart's side.

"I'll find your folks," Louis whispered. "I'll tell them how brave you were." Louis looked at all the dark shapes around him. "Somebody'll come and bury you. Somebody'll come and bury you all."

"No, wait!" came a voice, making Louis jump. A hand clutched his ankle.

"Gah! What the devil!?"

At first he thought it was Stuart, come back from the dead to ask if Louis heard something rustling in the woods, but then Louis turned and saw another dark shape lying on the ground nearby, its dark arm snaking out to him, holding him so he couldn't get away.

"Don't bury me!" the thing squawked. "I ain't dead yet!"

Louis tried to pull away, but the thing held on like a viper.

"Get off! Get off!"

"Are you the Angel of Death?"

"What!? No, I'm—"

Louis's eyes adjusted and he could just make out the boy's gray uniform. He was a Confederate. He immediately thought of his gun, sitting against a tree miles away at the

Union camp. His eyes searched the darkness for a bayonet, a rifle, anything he could use to defend himself.

"Please," the Rebel said. "I don't know what's happened. Why is it so dark and quiet?"

"It's the middle of the night," Louis said. "That's what happens at night. It gets dark."

"Are you a medic? Can you take me back to my regiment?"

"What? Take you back to your regiment?" Couldn't the fool see Louis was a Yankee? "I'm not a—"

The Rebel's head turned this way and that, like he couldn't see a thing. It was dark, but not that dark. Louis bent low and waved a hand in front of the soldier's face. He was blind as a bat, his face and eyes charred like the inside of a furnace.

"You're not a what?" the Confederate asked. "Are you still there?"

"Of course I'm here," Louis told him. "You've got hold of my leg."

The Rebel let go and Louis stepped back out of his reach, trying to think what to do.

"Sorry. It's just—it's so dark. And my head hurts. Can you take me back to my regiment? Are they far gone?"

Louis studied the Rebel. He could see now he was around his own age, maybe even younger, and his gray Confederate uniform looked three sizes too big. His blind eyes searched the darkness eagerly, hoping for some shape or shadow that might give him his bearings.

Louis considered his options. He could leave the boy, which didn't seem right, or kill him, which might have been a mercy but was out of the question. During the heat of battle, killing another man was one thing. It was kill or be killed, and both sides accepted that. Killing this boy here and now would be akin to murder—even if he might have been the one to take Stuart down in cold blood.

An idea struck Louis. Why not take him back to the Union camp as a prisoner of war, maybe see if he could get a promotion out of it? Even on the eve of going home, a promotion would mean a better pension, which his family could sorely use. But without a weapon, how to convince the Reb to come with him?

"All right. On your feet," Louis said. "We're . . . we're going to find your regiment."

The boy was so profuse in his thanks Louis began to feel sorry for the lie, but there was no other choice.

"Try to find my pack," the boy said. "It's just inside the wood line. It's the one with the baseball bat in it."

Louis paused.

"The what?"

"The baseball bat. It's a white haversack with the handle sticking out. I left it near an oak tree."

Louis slipped away and found a white oak a few paces into the woods. Behind it was a haversack, just as the boy had said, a bat handle sticking up out of the top. Louis slid it out to have a look. It was the finest bat he had ever seen. Not a broom handle or a whittled-down tree limb, but a real, honest-to-God lathe-turned hickory bat, such as Louis had only seen in the hands of the finest players on the Excelsiors. The barrel was heavy and perfectly smooth, and the long handle had a knob at the end to keep it in the batter's hands as he swung. Louis took a practice swing with it right there in the forest, enjoying the *whhht* it made and the power it held.

He brought the bat and the sack back to the boy, who was sitting up now. He had his hands in front of his eyes, but turned at the sound of Louis's approach.

"I'm blind, ain't I?"

"I think so," Louis told him.

The boy sobbed once. "My rifle. It exploded. I remember now. I never even got a shot off. My rifle blew up in my face. The next thing I knew, I woke up here, in the dark, and I heard your voice. Are you—are you a surgeon?"

"No. They've come and gone. I just came back to find a friend of mine."

Louis's hand found the ball in his pocket.

"Where'd you get this bat?" he asked.

The boy was crying now. Not hard tears. Soft ones, like he'd just lost a friend. "My pa. He's—he's a carpenter. He makes them for some of the boys who play."

"I've never seen its equal," Louis told him. He sat down on the grass next to the Reb.

"I was going to be mustered out tomorrow," the boy said through his tears. "Go back to Louisville."

"Me too!" Louis said. "Mustered out, I mean."

"Where are you from?"

"Um—farther north," said Louis.

"What, like . . . Nashville?"

Louis didn't have the faintest idea where Nashville was. "Close to," he said.

The boy dried his eyes and Louis clapped him on the shoulder.

"All right then. On your feet. We've got a train to catch."

3

The boy's name was Jeremiah Walker, and he played second base.

"I swear, I've seen him do it!" Louis told him.

"Look, I may be blind," Jeremiah said, "but you can't tell me nobody ever made a baseball curve."

"I'm telling you—his name is Candy Cummings. He's one of the boys comes round to play ball with us. Lives out near Red Hook. He got to throwing clam shells on a curve one day and reckoned he could do the same thing with a ball."

They passed the spot on the road where Louis had met the corporal, and he knew they had a mile yet to go. He was enjoying the baseball talk so much he almost hated to get there.

"Clam shells?" Jeremiah said.

"I swear. I saw him skunk some of the best hitters in . . . my hometown." Louis had come dangerously close to saying Brooklyn, and he worried now that Jeremiah might have heard of Red Hook. He'd have to be more careful.

"You only count catches on the fly, right?" he asked.

"'Course. Though there's some that still play off the bounce. They ain't finding too many takers, though."

"Back home," Louis said, careful not to give anything away, "there were only three clubs that played that way when I left. I expect they've given it up by now."

"How many unhittable balls do you allow before you grant the batter first base?"

"Three," Louis told him.

"Your umpires count every pitch?"

"No. Just when things start to get out of hand one way or the other."

"What about bunting?" Jeremiah asked. "Do your teams look upon it favorably, or—"

Louis put out a hand to stop the Confederate.

"What? What is it?" Jeremiah said.

Louis hadn't heard anything and he hadn't seen anything. Instead he was beginning to wonder if there wasn't something else he should do with Jeremiah. He couldn't believe he was even considering it, but he knew in his heart he could not take the second baseman in as a prisoner of war. Not even for a promotion.

"I think we need to turn here," he said. He led Jeremiah off into the woods and circled around.

"Isn't this—isn't this the direction we just came from?" Jeremiah asked.

"Hey, who's the one with the eyes here? Trust me."

Jeremiah got quiet, but soon they were talking baseball again as Louis guided them through the woods. He eventually found a wide, dark field with trampled grass, which meant either the Army of Northern Virginia or a herd of elephants had come this way. Though he knew it was crazy, Louis followed the trail.

The two walked for hours, never running out of baseball talk. They had just begun discussing the merits of stealing bases when a voice in the darkness interrupted them.

"Who comes there?"

Neither of them spoke, and Jeremiah nudged Louis.

"Uh, friend!" Louis said.

The sentry waited. Louis heard a rustling. "And the countersign, friend?"

Jeremiah turned his blind eyes toward Louis like he was waiting for him to answer.

"Jeremiah," Louis whispered. "I can't—I don't know—"

A confused look passed over his friend's face, then Jeremiah turned toward the voice in the darkness and said, "Blueberry pie, friend."

There was a pause, and Louis waited for the lead to start flying if Jeremiah's memory had gotten knocked to Tuesday when his rifle exploded.

"Advance friend, blueberry pie," came the response. There was more rustling, which Louis took to mean they were no longer in the sentry's sights. "Need a hand there?"

"No!" Louis and Jeremiah said together, and too quickly.

"No," Jeremiah said. "Thank you kindly. We're not bad off, just got a little . . . turned around on the way home."

"Godspeed," the sentry told them. "And be a little quicker with the countersign next time, boys. There's Yankees on sacred soil."

"We will, sir. Thank you," Jeremiah said. He nudged Louis and they were off, giving the picket a wide berth.

When they were a little ways into the woods, Louis spoke.

"I uh, I don't know what I was thinking. I must have forgotten the password."

"I think I can forgive my guardian angel that one transgression," Jeremiah said.

Louis stopped him. The time for lies was at an end. "Jeremiah, I'm not an angel. I'm a devil. A Red-Legged Devil. I'm not a Reb, Jeremiah—I'm a Yankee."

Jeremiah didn't look as shocked as Louis thought he would be.

"I know," he said.

"You know? What, because I didn't know the countersign?"

Jeremiah pulled away from Louis and reached out until he found a tree to anchor himself.

"I don't figure it's something you'll ever need to know," he said, "but Nashville is *south* of Louisville. By a far piece. Any Southern boy'd know that. Heck, an Ohioan would know that."

"Right," Louis said, disappointed he hadn't known.

"And you ain't gonna find too many clam shells anywhere but the ocean, and you didn't say you was from Charleston or some such."

"I could have been from Norfolk! That's on the ocean, isn't it?"

"And I don't know what city you're from where 'only' three teams still count fly outs on the bounce. There ain't but four teams in Louisville, perhaps ten in all of Kentucky."

"Okay, okay. I get it. As a spy I'm not worth a plugged nickel."

"Not only that," Jeremiah said, "you talk like a Yankee."

"Oh yeah? Well, you talk like a cotton-picking Rebel!"

Louis and Jeremiah laughed, then grew quiet.

"What I can't figure," Jeremiah said, "is what we're doing at the edge of the Confederate army camp. When I had you pegged for a Yank, I thought for sure we were off to your side, not mine."

"Why come along then?" Louis asked.

Jeremiah shrugged. "I can't see. What was I going to do? Clonk you on the head and set out on my own? I figured a Union prison camp was better than running into trees until a bear ate me."

"That was the plan. A prison camp, I mean. Then I changed my mind."

"Why?"

"I don't know. You were going home tomorrow and so was

I, and . . . well, I guess I figured anybody that liked baseball that much couldn't be too bad a person, Reb or not."

Jeremiah fumbled with his sack and withdrew his baseball bat.

"If you've a mind to clonk me now," Louis told him, "I think it only fair to remind you that I *can* see you coming."

Jeremiah smiled. "Here," he said, holding the bat out to Louis. He meant for him to have it.

"No. I couldn't," Louis told him. "Your pa made that."

"And just what am I going to do with it?" he asked. "Go on, take it. This whole thing—this whole thing was a mistake to begin with. We weren't supposed to fire, you know. We were just watching the game on a lark. Then Samuels got twitchy and went and shot that boy, the center fielder. It wasn't right, but we had to take it up then, or else have you boys on our heels."

"Look, maybe it's just a flash burn," Louis said. "You might get your sight back after a time. Then you'll need that bat again."

"If that happens, my pa can make me another. Here. Take this back to—what, New York?"

"No! *Pfft.* Not New York. *Brooklyn.*"

"Is that close to Nashville?" Jeremiah asked.

"Very nearly," Louis said, smiling.

"Here." Jeremiah stepped forward until Louis had to take the bat or be struck by it.

"Wait, I'll trade you," Louis told him. He hesitated a

moment, then pulled his father's baseball from his pocket and put it in Jeremiah's hand. The Rebel turned it over, feeling the surface of it.

"This is a fine baseball."

"The finest," Louis said. "My pa made that when he was a boy."

"Sounds like you don't want to part with it."

"It's my good luck charm," Louis told him. "But I think you need it more than me."

"You sure about that? Looked around at where you're at lately?"

Louis smiled. "I'll be all right. I'm going home tomorrow, and I'm not going to let anybody stop me."

Jeremiah held out a hand and they shook as friends.

"Too bad we couldn't have settled this whole thing over a game of baseball," Louis told him, "trading fly balls instead of lead ones."

"Better for your side we didn't," Jeremiah said. "You'd have lost for sure."

"Oho!"

"You'd best be heading on," Jeremiah told him. "I can make it from here."

Louis looked about at the forest. It had started to glow with the first hint of morning.

"I think you'll be bouncing off the trees from here to Richmond," Louis told him. "Better let me take you a little farther in."

This time Louis kept his eye out for sentries and spotted a campfire through the bracken before the picket spotted them. The boys shook hands once more and took their leave, Louis with a new hickory bat, Jeremiah with a new baseball. Louis hoped his father would understand, and he suspected he would.

Over his shoulder he heard Jeremiah Walker call to the sentries for help, and Louis took off for Brooklyn as fast as his red devil legs could carry him.

Third Inning: A Ballad of the Republic

Brooklyn, New York, 1894

1

"I'm Cap Anson!" one boy called.

"I'm Oyster Burns!" said another.

The boys had rechristened Pigtown the Polo Grounds, and now they were giving themselves upgrades by pretending to be their favorite players.

"I'm Fred Pfeffer!" Tommy Collum said.

"Fred Pfeffer, Fred Pfeffer," sang Joseph, the biggest of the boys. "With him it's always Fred Pfeffer. He's like an el conductor. 'Tickets please. Tickets. Where's your tickets? Tickets.' Same thing over and over."

They all had a laugh. On the edge of the group Arnold Schneider laughed with them.

"I'll be King Kelly," he said.

"King Kelly!?" Joseph said. "Does he even *play* anymore?"

"He played for the New York Giants last year!" Arnold said. "He turned a triple play against Brooklyn."

"Yeah, so did my gran," Joseph said. The boys all had another laugh. "All right, me and George choose up sides."

One by one all the boys were chosen by the captains. All the boys but Arnold. He was the smallest and worst player there, and he knew it, but he still watched the captains, hoping one of them would take him today.

"You bring that good bat, Arnie?" Joseph asked.

"No. That bat's my dad's. He got it—"

"In the war. Yeah, yeah, we know. You want to play, you bring that bat next time."

"But with me the teams are even," Arnold said.

"He's right," said George. Arnold's heart leaped.

"Here, catch," George said. He threw the ball to Arnold, but it was too far over his head. Another boy caught it and threw it back.

"Here you go, Arnie."

The ball sailed over his head again. And again. Arnold knew this game. They were playing keep-away. He stopped trying to catch the ball and glared at them, his hands clenched and his fists shaking.

"Boat-lickers," he said.

"Oooooh," Joseph laughed. "I'm soooo scared."

Arnold wanted to cry, but he would never do that again. Not in front of the boys. Instead he walked away as fast as he could.

"Good-bye, King Kelly!" Joseph taunted, and Arnold broke into a run.

When Arnold finally slowed down to wipe the tears off his face he realized he had run halfway up Bedford Avenue.

He was in the Eastern District with the vaudeville theaters. He passed Hyde & Behman's and the Empire Theater, stopping to read the placards outside announcing the nightly acts. Above him, the Broadway–Brooklyn line rattled by on its elevated platform, and he watched as ladies and gentlemen in their fine clothes went scurrying for shop awnings to escape the soot and smoke that drifted down from the train.

Electric lights hummed at the entrance of the Gayety Theater, and a name on the board outside caught Arnold's eye as he passed. He rushed back to read the sign:

"Appearing all this week: O'Dowd's Neighbors! Featuring Weber and Field, Dutch Knockabouts; Haines and Vidocq, back talkers; the Braatz Brothers, acrobats; John LeClair, balancer and juggler; Drummond and Tahley, musicians; Alice Raymond, cornet player; Mike 'King' Kelly, famed baseballer; William Wheatman, maker of faces . . ."

Mike "King" Kelly, famed baseballer! Arnold couldn't believe it. King Kelly? Here, in Brooklyn? On the vaudeville stage? He rushed to the door to look inside, but he only saw the lobby. The doorman eyed him and he rushed back to the sign. "Mike 'King' Kelly, famed baseballer." Why had they buried him so far down the list of performers? Wouldn't he be the star attraction?

Admission was fifty cents, and Arnold didn't have to pat his pockets to know he didn't have enough coins. There was no chance his parents would give him money for a vaudeville show either. They wouldn't even like that he'd been in the theater district.

Music and laughter trickled out of the Gayety Theater. The show had already started. Arnold *had* to see King Kelly.

There was only one thing for it. He'd have to sneak in.

A group of young men and their ladies came strutting down the lane and stopped to consider the playbill. They would be perfect. Arnold tried to watch them without being obvious about it, silently willing them to decide to take in the show. A well-timed outburst of laughter sold them on the matter, and they moved as one toward the doorway where the men made a great show of paying their ladies' way in. Being on the short end of ten, Arnold slipped around them out of sight of the ticket seller and ducked inside.

The theater was little more than half full, and Arnold slunk down a side aisle and slid into a seat. He waited for someone to point a finger, to grab him by the shoulder, but no one seemed to have noticed he'd snuck in, and he relaxed. King Kelly wasn't on the stage now anyway—it was an acrobat routine with trained tumblers. After that came a man and a woman who played violins, then a face contortionist who made Arnold laugh, and a comedian who did not. He began to fear he had missed King Kelly entirely, when the master of ceremonies stepped onto the stage to announce the next act.

"Ladies and gentlemen," the emcee said, "the Gayety Theater is now proud to present that legendary Rascal of Round Ball, that Scoundrel of Swat, the Dandy of the Diamond—Mr. Mike 'King' Kelly in, 'He Would Be an Actor, or, The Ballplayer's Revenge'!"

King Kelly pranced out onto the stage with a glass of beer in one hand and a baseball bat in the other. It was him, sure enough. He wore the blue and white uniform of the Boston Beaneaters and a bright red scarf tied under his collar. His dark black hair was smoothed back under his white cap, and his big bushy mustache had just a hint of curl at the ends.

Kelly drew a polite smattering of applause and Arnold leaned forward in his seat.

"Ah, it's great to be back here in Brooklyn," Kelly said, his Irish accent rolling off his tongue. "Why, it was here, against your very own Brooklyn Bridegrooms, that I robbed Monte Ward of a home run. I remember that day very clearly," he said, settling in to a story he'd clearly told many times. "'Twas getting on toward dusk when Monte stepped to the plate, and we all knew the umpire would soon call the game on account of darkness. But the score was tied two apiece, you see, and the Grooms had something cooking with two outs in the ninth. Pinckney and O'Brien stood on second and third, and a hit of any kind would send us packing back to Beantown."

Kelly took a long draw off his beer, but not so long as to lose the audience.

"Now, it's gotten so dark I can hardly see Clarkson on the

73

mound, let alone the batter. But I hear the crack of the bat and see the infielders turn, and I know a scorching sphere is headed my way. I go back, back, back into the big vast swirling darkness of Eastern Park—you lot have been there, so you know what I mean—and I reach out as high as I can and I *jump* as high as I can," Kelly said, pantomiming the catch as best he could with his beer in lieu of a glove, "and I come down with me hand raised high in the twilight, dashing the hopes of the Brooklyn faithful!"

The hometown crowd gave him a good-natured boo, and he smiled.

"'Out number three!' yells the ump. 'Game called on account of darkness!' So I run back to the dugout with me glove closed tight, and our manager, old Frank Selee, comes forward with the rest of the boys to congratulate me. 'Kel,' says he, 'that was the finest catch I've ever yet seen.'

"'And you still haven't,' says I, and I opened my glove. There wasn't a thing in it. The ball went a mile over me head!"

What a marvelous trick! Arnold clapped himself silly, and the audience roared with laughter. Kelly saluted them all with his beer.

"Tell us about the ten-thousand-dollar transfer!" someone yelled.

"What'd you do with all that money?" called another.

"I ate strawberries and ice cream every day," Kelly said with a grin.

"Yeah, and the bartenders got the rest!" someone heckled.

Kelly told a few more stories from his playing days, then recited "Casey at the Bat," changing out mighty Casey's name for his own. When he was finished, he left the stage to the sound of the house band playing "Slide, Kelly, Slide" and great applause.

Not even the promise of the Salambos, fire-handlers from Brazil, could keep Arnold in his seat. He dashed down the aisle and out of the theater, turning down the side alley where he hoped King Kelly would emerge. He guessed the wrong alley, though, and by the time he had run around to the other side King Kelly and another man were already halfway to the street.

"Mr. Kelly!" Arnold called. "King! King! How about an autograph!"

Kelly stopped and turned, smiling magnificently.

"One of me fans, Hiroshi!" he said to the other man. Arnold slid to a stop in front of them, and he could see now Kelly was accompanied by an Oriental—a Chinaman or some such—dressed in brightly colored silks and sporting a braided ponytail like a girl might wear. There was something crawling on the man's right shoulder, and Arnold jumped in fright as a black monkey leaped from the Oriental onto Kelly's back.

"Me gentleman's gentleman," Kelly said. "Me valet Hiroshi. Now laddie, what's your name?"

"A—Arnold," he said. "Arnold Schneider."

"Right. Now, let's see here." He searched the pockets of

his coat. "Aha. Here's me fountain pen then. What have you got for me to sign, Arthur?"

Arnold's heart sank. Here was King Kelly before him, ready to sign his famous autograph, and Arnold had nothing in his pocket but three pennies and a bit of fluff. Now the boys at Pigtown would never believe him.

"It's—it's Arnold, sir. And I'm sorry, but I don't—"

Arnold stopped. Kelly suddenly had the most peculiar look on his face, like he had fallen asleep with his eyes open. The ballplayer's face lost all expression and his body began to sway.

"Mr. Kelly, are you all right?"

Hiroshi tried to catch Kelly before he fell, but he was too late. The monkey jumped from the sinking ship and King Kelly dove headlong into the gutter, splashing face-first into the muck.

Arnold rushed to Kelly's side and tried to turn him over.

"What's happened!? What should I do? Should I go for a doctor?" Arnold asked. He looked up at Hiroshi's blank face and realized he probably didn't understand a word Arnold was saying. "I—I'm sorry," Arnold said loudly. *"No speak Chinaman."*

Hiroshi sighed. "I'm Japanese," he said with a distinct New England accent. "And no, he doesn't need a doctor. He needs a paddy wagon. King Kelly is drunk."

2

Arnold and Hiroshi carried the unconscious Kelly back to his boardinghouse, though to call his temporary place of residence a "boardinghouse" was generous. It was unclean and overcrowded, what Arnold's father would probably call a "flophouse." A man behind a counter shielded by chicken wire watched the three of them suspiciously as they crossed the lobby, and Arnold kept his head down as they dragged Kelly toward the stairs.

"Does King Kelly really stay here?" Arnold asked Hiroshi.

The valet grunted. "If they haven't thrown his bags into the alley yet."

"No pets!" the man behind the chicken wire yelled. Hiroshi stopped and clicked some command to the monkey, and it leaped down and scurried out the front door and into the night.

"Wait, where will it—" Arnold started to ask, but Hiroshi was already moving again.

The stairs were just as full of people as the lobby, and

Arnold wondered if these were people who couldn't afford a proper room. Some slept; others stared into the dim haze of the place, not registering Arnold and the others as they passed.

At the second-floor landing, Kelly roused for a moment and seemed almost lucid.

"What's all this then?" he asked. He straightened, and Arnold and Hiroshi backed away, watching to see if he could stand. He noticed neither of them, instead focusing on a homeless man huddled in the stairwell corner.

"You look a mite cold, friend," Kelly said. He struggled with his long coat, the removal of his arms giving him particular problems in his inebriated state. Arnold noticed that Hiroshi made no move to help him. At length Kelly escaped his coat and ceremoniously draped it over the man in the corner.

Kelly turned to his valet and smiled.

"Very noble, sir," Hiroshi told him, though his tone said he thought otherwise.

"And what's your name, laddie?" Kelly asked.

"Arnold—" he began to tell him again, but Kelly's eyes lost their focus again and he fell forward. Arnold was relieved when Hiroshi put a hand to Kelly's chest and stopped his fall, but was equally horrified when the manservant pushed him hard the other way, sending Kelly crashing to the stairs.

Arnold stared at Hiroshi in disbelief, but the manservant said nothing, simply taking one of Kelly's hands and dragging him up the stairs. Arnold rushed to help, doing his best to keep King Kelly's head from *thunk-thunk-thunking* on the stair treads.

King Kelly's room was tiny, even smaller than the one Arnold had all to himself at home. There was little more than a bed in one corner and a chair in another, the washroom shared by all somewhere else down the hall. Broken plaster hung from the ceiling, and the room smelled of sweat, liquor, and vomit.

Hiroshi went to the window, wrenched it open, and whistled. Arnold thought this very odd, until the little black monkey leaped in, having somehow scaled the outside of the building. The valet gave the creature a bit of treat from his pocket, then settled into the chair.

Arnold looked around the room and shook his head. "I thought he lived on strawberries and ice cream."

The manservant laughed. "Maybe once. He talks like he still does, just like he keeps me around, to make people think he's still rich. But he squandered all his money, and now he keeps himself in booze and pays my meager salary with these vaudeville shows. That coat he so generously gave away just now was the only one of its kind he owned. Now the poor mick'll freeze to death before he drinks himself to death."

"Begging your pardon, sir," Arnold said, "but you don't sound much like a Japanner."

The valet rubbed his face in his hands. "I lived in Boston

for twenty-five years before this sot hired me to carry his bags for him."

"Shouldn't we get him up off the floor?" Arnold asked.

Hiroshi afforded his employer a disdainful look and went back to feeding the monkey. "Have at it," he said.

Kelly was slight for a man, but Arnold still had trouble hefting him up off the floor. He started with his head and arms, then tried lifting him from the waist, turning his body sideways to roll it onto the mattress. Hiroshi did nothing to help. Just when Arnold though he had Kelly's lower half securely on the bed his top half slid off and *thunked* to the floor.

Kelly woke with a start.

"That is a smashing hat," he said.

Arnold blinked, then put a hand to his head. He was just wearing an ordinary boy's cap.

"Smashing hat," Kelly said. He started to giggle. He righted himself and plucked Arnold's hat from his head, then stood and smashed the cap beneath his heel. "*Smashing . . .* hat!" He laughed, then spied his own top hat, which had fallen to the floor.

"*Smashing hat!*" he cried, putting his foot through the top of his own hat. As strange as it all was, Arnold couldn't help but laugh with him.

Kelly's eyes fixed on the bowler his manservant wore.

"No," the valet warned.

"Smashing hat, Hiroshi!" said Kelly, and he chased the

Japanese man around the room. The monkey flew screeching from Hiroshi's shoulders and perched on the bed, and the neighbors pounded on the wall for them all to be quiet. Kelly made a swipe for Hiroshi's hat, but the manservant was too quick for him. To save his hat, Hiroshi took it off and tossed it through the open window.

"There. No smashing my hat," he said.

Kelly went to the window and leaned out.

"You've lost your hat, my good man. Just let me fetch it for you—"

King Kelly had a leg out the window before Arnold and Hiroshi grabbed him and pulled him back inside. Kelly fought them the whole time, as though he had no idea what peril it would be to fall three stories to the street.

When they'd pulled him a sufficient distance away from the window, Hiroshi reared back and slapped Kelly hard across the face. Kelly had certainly been silly, but Arnold couldn't believe how cruel his manservant was. Neither could King Kelly.

"What on Earth—what did you strike me for?"

"You just tried to jump out the window."

That thought, more than the slap, seemed to sober Kelly up. The red color drained out of his face and he slumped on the bed, looking around as though seeing the room for the first time.

"Who are you, laddie?" he asked Arnold. "What's your name?"

Arnold told him again.

"I'll get you some coffee," Hiroshi said.

"No, no," Kelly said. "I feel fine. Fit as a fiddle." He stood. "Why, I haven't felt this good since I won the batting title with Chicago. What year was that, Hiroshi?"

The valet was at the window, trying to see where his hat had fallen. "You know darn well what year it was."

"1886," said Arnold. "You hit .388. You also led the league in runs for the third straight year."

"Say, I like this lad!" Kelly said. "Aye, 1886 it was. The season old Cap Anson had those Pinkerton boys follow me about. I grew so tired of private eyes watching me every move that I decked one at the train station before I alighted. It wasn't 'til we were back in Chicago I found the poor lad wasn't really a detective. That was my last season with the White Stockings to be sure!"

"They sold you to Boston for ten thousand dollars," Arnold said.

"Aye, made A. G. Spalding a great deal of money, I did."

"You made a fair bit yourself," Hiroshi said from his chair in the corner. "And just where is that two-thousand-dollar salary now? The three-thousand-dollar 'bonus' for the use of your likeness? The endorsement fees for the King Kelly bats, the 'Slide, Kelly, Slide' sled, the shoe polish with your name on the can?"

"You know," Kelly told Arnold, ignoring his manservant, "I was once given a silver bat by the *Cincinnati Enquirer* when I played in the Queen City, in honor of hitting the first home run at the Avenue Grounds. That very bat is still on display in a store window in me hometown of Paterson, New Jersey."

Hiroshi gave a short, harsh laugh. Arnold didn't understand what was so funny about that, but Kelly didn't seem to mind. He wobbled back and forth, then caught himself like he was trying to stay awake.

"Have ye—have ye ever heard the story of how I substituted meself for Dimples Tate while he was trying to catch a foul ball?"

"Why don't you tell him the story of how you hit .189 your final season with Boston?" his valet asked. "Or how you made ten errors in just eighteen games last year with the Giants?"

But everything Hiroshi said was lost on Kelly. He was fast asleep again, sprawled out on his bed. The Japanese manservant buried his head in his hands.

"If you hate him so much, why are you still here?" Arnold asked.

"That's a very good question."

Hiroshi got up from his chair and called the monkey to him with a whistle. He pulled a suitcase out from under the bed, opened it to check the contents, then stood.

"You're—you're *leaving?*" Arnold asked.

"Might as well. Kelly can't pay his rent, let alone me. I'm going back to Boston."

"But what about next season?"

"There isn't going to *be* a next season, kid. Not for King Kelly, not on the baseball diamond. He hasn't told anyone, but the Giants cut him. Not even his old friend Monte Ward will have him. He's finished."

"But the stage, the vaudeville halls. People will still pay to hear his stories."

"Anson, hat. Fetch my hat," Hiroshi said, and the little monkey leaped to the open window and was gone.

"Kelly barely makes enough on the stage to keep him in beer and cigarettes," the valet told Arnold. "He drinks more than he earns every night. He's not the ten-thousand-dollar beauty anymore, but he still lives like it."

Hiroshi was clearly done with Kelly, but all Arnold could think about were the records the old ballplayer had broken, the songs that were sung about him, the picture of King Kelly sliding into second that had replaced the pictures of Custer's Last Stand in every public house in Brooklyn.

Anson the monkey climbed back into the room with Hiroshi's hat. The valet took it from him and dusted it off.

"That silver bat he won," Arnold said, still staring at Kelly. "You laughed. Did he really not win it?"

"Oh, he won it all right, and it's right there in a shop window in Paterson for all the world to see, just like he said. Only the shop is R. J. Robinson's Pawnbroker and Loan. He sold it to pay his bar tab." Hiroshi put his hat on his head and opened the door to leave. "*Sayonara*, kid. The job's yours now. And tell Kelly he can keep the monkey."

✢ ✢ ✢

Water sloshed onto King Kelly's face and he sat up like a man stuck with a pin.

"Whaaaa—! Who? What?" he sputtered.

Arnold felt a little bad for dumping a bucket of cold water on him, but didn't figure he had much other choice. He flipped the bucket over and sat down on it next to Kelly.

"I'm dreadful sorry to have to wake you like that," Arnold said.

"W—what day is it?" Kelly asked.

"Saturday." The monkey jumped on Kelly's back and perched there.

"And where am I?"

"A boardinghouse."

"I meant what city, laddie."

"Oh. Brooklyn."

Kelly put a hand to his head, as though it pained him to think.

"Ah. Yes. Brooklyn. And you are—?"

"Arnold, sir. Arnold Schneider."

Arnold waited for some sort of recognition to dawn on Kelly's face, but it didn't.

"I met you last night," Arnold told him. "I asked you for your autograph."

"Well, I certainly hope ye haven't been waiting all this time to get it."

"No. I came back to help you out." Arnold stood. "I'm your new valet."

"Are you now? And just what's happened to Hiroshi then?"

"He went back to Boston."

Kelly nodded. "So. You're me new valet, eh? And just how old *are* you?"

"Ten," Arnold told him.

"Aha. And what is our first order of business today, laddie?"

"To get you cleaned up."

✤ ✤ ✤

Arnold waited outside the Turkish bath in Brooklyn Heights with Anson the monkey for what seemed like hours. Kelly's treatment had cost Arnold a fair bit of what little money he'd saved for himself, but it was necessary. While Kelly'd been inside, Arnold had run the ballplayer's shirt, pants, and collar down the street to have them cleaned with kerosene at the dry cleaner too.

After a time Kelly strolled out of the bathhouse looking positively regal. His face was flush, his hair was slicked back, and his mustache stood at attention.

Anson jumped from Arnold's shoulder to his master's.

"I don't believe I have ever sweat so much in me entire life," Kelly said. "All right, valet. You've got the whisky wrung out of me, and me clothes have never looked finer." He straightened the red handkerchief tied around his newly pressed collar. "Where to next? Have I an audition at Prospect Hall?"

"No," Arnold told him. "You're playing Pigtown."

3

Arnold Schneider was a hero.

Just about every boy in Brooklyn heard that King Kelly was at the Pigtown field, and they rushed down to crowd him and pepper the baseball star with a thousand questions. Kelly answered them all with a wide smile, though just slightly smaller than the smile Arnold was wearing.

"What was it like winning the pennant?"

"Which time?" Kelly asked.

"The first time."

"With Boston!"

"Tell us about being sold for ten thousand dollars!"

"What'd you do with the money, Kel?"

"What's your monkey's name?"

"Anson," he managed.

"You mean like Cap Anson? What was it like to play with him?"

"Oh, he's a tough player, all right, but an even tougher manager. The first day of practice he ordered me to lose twenty pounds and put me through the mill with special meals and supervised dog trots. 'Course I have a new boss now," King Kelly said. He smashed Arnold's hat farther down on his head and rubbed it around. "This one's got me cleaned up and living straight again."

For the first time in his life, everybody wanted to stand near Arnold, to talk with him, to be his best friend. He was giddy with the rush of it all.

"Tell us about Corcoran," one of the boys begged Kelly.

"And George Gore!"

"What about Fred Pfeffer?" Tommy Collum said.

"*Fred Pfeffer, Fred Pfeffer!*" Arnold taunted, and everyone laughed. They laughed!

"Ah, now Freddy was a great friend of mine," Kelly told them. "A great friend indeed. He and I used to go out drinking, ah . . . *lemonade.*" Kelly smiled. "Freddy was a proponent of 'inside baseball.' Do ye know what that is? So-called 'scientific baseball.' He even wrote a book on it."

The boys begged Kelly to show them how it was done, and he asked for a bat and ball. Arnold handed him his own bat, the one his father had brought home from the Civil War.

"Now this here is a fine bat, a fine bat indeed," Kelly said, weighing it in his hands. He stood back from the boys and gave it a swing. "Trade you me glove for it, Arnold."

The boys gasped as Kelly gave Arnold his baseball mitt.

It was thick and padded like a pillow, the kind that was in fashion among the catchers in the National League. Arnold marveled at it. None of the boys could afford a proper glove like this. It was heavy, like a great mitten with a leather-clad lump of stuffing forming a U along the base of the palm. Where the broad thumb met the rest of the mitt there were two small strings of leather to hold them together. The other boys watched on quietly as Arnold put his hand inside the massive thing. He was just able to bend it along its middle, and for a moment he imagined himself clamping down tight on an Amos Rusie fastball.

"Marvelous piece o' cowhide, ain't it?" Kelly said. "A trade then?"

"I—I can't," Arnold said, and he told Kelly the story of how his father had traded for the bat during the war. He sighed and handed the glove back. "I wish I could," he said.

"Ah well, you can have me glove anyway, laddie. No trade."

Arnold felt the wave of envy from the boys around him, and he knew he would never be picked last again. Ever.

Kelly put Arnold behind the plate and arranged the rest of the boys all around the infield.

"Scientific baseball is about playing the percentages, see?" Kelly said. "If you know Oyster Burns always pulls to the left side, why, you tell your fielders to shift that direction. If

Big Dan Brouthers likes to give the ball a Baltimore chop, you play your boys in, see? That's scientific."

Kelly showed the boys how to drill themselves on the basics of inside baseball, then taught them a few tricks they wouldn't find in any book: how to fool base runners into thinking you'd overthrown their bag when there was really an outfielder standing behind them to catch it, how to keep an extra ball in your pocket in case you lost one over your head, and how to skip bases when the umpires weren't looking. After that they played a few innings until Anson the monkey snatched up the ball and led the boys on a wild chase for it all over Pigtown.

"I've had a fine time, laddie," Kelly told Arnold, "but I'd best be getting back. I've a show to do tonight, and I find me act goes better when I've had a little something to drink first. And I don't mean lemonade. I'll tell you, lad, I'd rather face ten thousand angry baseball enthusiasts on the diamond field than go before a friendly audience in a theater."

"Kel, is it true what your valet said? That you won't play again next season?"

"Not won't, laddie. Can't. I'd play if I could, but no one will have me."

"But you're not old. Cap Anson's older than you are and he's still playing first base for the White Stockings."

Kelly sighed as the boys laughed and scrambled across the field after the monkey.

"I don't know how he does it, laddie. Cap Anson. Truly I don't. They keep moving the mound around for starters, and the pitchers don't throw underhanded anymore. Nowadays it comes in hard and fast, kicking and screaming into the catcher's mitt. Amos Rusie, Cy Young, Kid Nichols—pitchers are bigger and stronger and wickeder than ever before. And they hurt like hell to catch, by the way, even with all o' that padding. And now I hear they're actually thinking of counting foul balls as strikes. Mark my words: There won't be a batting average over .250 in all the league." He shook his head. "Baseball tain't like it were in the olden days, laddie. Me days of playing in the big leagues are through. It's the stage for me now, even though I'm not on Broadway. Heck, I'm in Brooklyn and I'm not even playing Prospect Hall."

King Kelly whistled and Anson broke off his game of keep-away and came scurrying back with the boys behind him.

"Time for me to be off, lads," Kelly told them. There was a general moan, but it turned into well-wishes and good-byes soon enough, and then calls for a new game when Kelly had gone.

"Me and Arnold are captains!" Joseph called.

Arnold knew he should have felt triumphant. He was a legend. He had brought King Kelly, the Ten-Thousand-Dollar Beauty, to Pigtown. But how long would it last? How long before he was little "Arnie" again, picked last every game and only allowed to play because of his bat—and now his glove. When the excitement of King Kelly went away, what would be left?

There was only one thing for it, he decided. King Kelly would have to stay.

The sun was just setting over the towers of the Brooklyn Bridge as Arnold made his way north toward Bushwick. He couldn't wait to tell Kelly his news.

"And now the pitcher holds the ball," he said, repeating lines from "Casey at the Bat." "And now he lets it go."

He stopped mid-run and took a swing with his father's bat. "And now the air is shattered by the force of Kelly's blow!"

He cheered for the hit—Kelly had gotten a double, not struck out like Casey had—then broke into a jog the rest of the way to the Gayety Theater, where King Kelly was appearing again that night. Three ladies with big poofy dresses were making their way inside when he arrived, and he slid in behind them. He had just stepped into the lobby when a hand grabbed him and yanked him back. The hand was attached to an ugly brute with a scraggy beard and a wandering eye.

"Awright. Let's have your ticket then, boy."

No! Arnold had to get inside to see King Kelly tonight. It couldn't wait. "I, uh—" he stammered, "I'm here to . . ." He looked down at the bat in his hands. "I'm here to bring King Kelly his bat!"

The ticket taker gave him a piercing look with his one good eye, then let him go.

"Shoulda used the stage door then," he said. "Kelly's backstage."

Arnold tipped his cap and ran to the front corner of the theater. Up on the stage he could feel the hot gas lights that burned along the edge, and he felt the eyes of the audience on him as though he might be some part of the act. He quickly ducked behind the heavy red curtain.

One of the Dutch Knockabouts pointed Arnold toward a room at the back of the theater where many of the acts were preparing to go onstage. Arnold cast about and finally found King Kelly in the corner, already dressed in his light blue Boston uniform and cap. As he approached, Arnold couldn't help imagining him in a different color uniform.

Kelly squinted as Arnold approached.

"Well, if it tain't me shadow!" He turned. "How the devil did you get down here, lad?"

"I told them I was here to bring you your bat for tonight's show," Arnold said. He handed him his father's bat, which Kelly again weighed appreciatively.

"Well, it's a fair sight better than the one they run me out there with." He nodded to a bat in the corner. "Give her a try."

Arnold picked up the bat. It was light as a feather.

"Stage prop," Kelly said. He took a drink from a glass sitting next to him, then refilled it from what looked like a whisky bottle. "Just a little something to fortify me for when I go out in front of the cranks," he explained. "I've always found that—"

"I've got you a tryout!" Arnold interrupted. He could contain himself no longer. "A tryout with the Brooklyn Bridegrooms!"

Kelly sat speechless for a moment.

"You, er, what?" he asked finally.

"I skipped out on the game at Pigtown after you left and I went to Eastern Park and talked to the Bridegrooms' manager, Foutz, while he was shagging fly balls in the outfield. He said for you to come by the field tomorrow before the game, and he'll see."

"He'll see . . . what?"

"You. In action. The way you played today at Pigtown, you're a far sight better than either of Brooklyn's catchers."

"That was against a bunch o' guttersnipes, laddie! Good as you lot are, you're hardly National League caliber."

"Game time is one o'clock," Arnold went on. "Foutz said to be there an hour before the game. You can even use my bat!"

Kelly stared at the bat in his hands. "Maybe . . . maybe I *could* still play. I did tell Monte I still had a few good seasons left in me, and I meant it."

"You'll be great, Kel. It'll be just like it was before. And you can come play ball with us at Pigtown some mornings. Not every morning, I know, because you'll have practice, but it'll be a kind of a practice, see?"

Kelly gave Arnold his big famous stage smile. "Sure, laddie. Absolutely. Just like it was before. You're a good kid, Arthur."

"Arnold."

Kelly picked up his glass and drank it in a single gulp.

"Arnold then," Kelly said. "You're a good lad, Arnold. But tell me. Promise me one thing, lad."

"Anything, Kel."

The ballplayer refilled his glass.

"I want you to promise me you'll never take a drink."

"Sure, Kel. Of course."

Kelly ignored his own advice and finished off another glass. His face twisted into a grimace, and Arnold watched him shiver as the drink went down.

"Better skedaddle, laddie. It's just about time for King Kelly's big act."

✢ ✢ ✢

Sunday morning Arnold ran all the way up Kings Highway and out to Eastern Park on the far side of town.

"I'm here with King Kelly!" he told the man at the ticket window, dashing inside before he could argue. Arnold had remembered to bring Kelly his father's bat the night before, but not Kelly's glove, and he'd need that for the tryout.

The Grooms were already taking batting practice, and Arnold searched for King Kelly and Dave "Scissors" Foutz, Brooklyn's left fielder and manager. He didn't see Kelly, but Foutz stood near the dugout making out a lineup card.

"Mr. Foutz! Mr. Foutz!" Arnold cried. The manager took a moment to recognize him from the day before and made his way over to the stands.

"Brought me Mike Kelly, have you?" Foutz said, his voice heavy with doubt.

"You mean he isn't here?" Arnold asked. It had to be past noon already. "He said he would be here. And he knows the way to the park. He's played here before."

"Look kid, I don't know if you're pulling my leg or if someone's pulling yours, but take my advice. Leave it alone. Even if Kelly could play, that man's got a monkey on his back."

"I know all about his monkey!" Arnold said. "The monkey's name is Cap Anson."

Dave Foutz had a good hard laugh at that, although Arnold didn't see what was so funny.

"That's good, kid. Maybe you do know him after all. But believe me: Kelly's through."

"No! He must have overslept is all," Arnold said, running up the aisle. "I'll have him here before game time!"

"Kid, wait!" Foutz yelled, but Arnold was already gone. Outside the park he hopped one of the trolleys heading west, paying a nickel for the privilege but saving much time. He hopped off near the Eastern District and dashed the rest of the way to Kelly's boardinghouse, ignoring the look of the man behind the chicken wire as he ran through the lobby and up the steps.

"Kel! Kel!" Arnold said, bursting into King Kelly's room. Only it wasn't King Kelly's room. A stranger rolled over in the bed, cursing at Arnold and throwing a shoe at him as he pulled the door closed. Did he have the wrong floor? The wrong room? He retraced his steps. No, this was the room Kelly had been staying in.

Back in the lobby Arnold went up to the man behind the screen.

"Do you know if King Kelly has changed rooms?"

The man put down his newspaper and frowned.

"You know Mike Kelly?"

"He's my friend," said Arnold.

"You know where he is?"

"No. I was hoping you could tell me."

The man harrumphed. "Well, your friend bailed owing me twelve dollars. Don't know how he got his things out with him, but he did. Must have climbed out the window. You gonna pay me the twelve dollars?"

"I—I don't have twelve dollars."

"Yeah. Right." The man flicked his newspaper back open. "You tell that bum he owes me twelve dollars."

Arnold ran to the theater. The story was the same there. "The louse slipped out after his last act owing more'n his pay in whisky," the stage manager told him. "If you're looking for him, I'd try any saloon in walking distance. Oh," he said before closing the door, "and tell him he won't be playing *any* stage in Brooklyn until he pays off what he owes."

There were a dozen or more bars in the Eastern District, and Arnold tried them all. In those that weren't empty or locked up tight he found some owner or barmaid who had heard of Kelly and seen him in the past week, but he had paid a call to none of their establishments last night. And every one of them was looking to settle up with him. One of them even handed Arnold Kelly's bar bill. It came to fifteen dollars and seventy-five cents.

Arnold walked back toward Kelly's boardinghouse in the vain hope that he might see Kelly, or one of the other performers, or find some clue as to where he'd gone. He had just resolved to return to the ballpark, thinking perhaps Kelly had only been late and they had missed each other, when an item in a shop window caught his eye.

It was his father's baseball bat. His father's baseball bat was in the window of a Fulton Street pawnbroker's shop.

Arnold burst into the store, almost tearing the bell on the door from its hinges. A stout man wearing a pin-striped vest and a large, thick mustache looked up from tinkering with a pocket watch.

"Looking for something in particular?" he asked.

"That bat in the window," Arnold said. "It's mine!"

The man smiled. "It's yours if you have fifty dollars."

"Fifty dollars!?"

"That bat is a collector's item," the man told him. "It's signed by King Kelly himself. Ever heard of him? He's a bit before your time, but he was one of the greats."

"No," Arnold said, though not in answer to the man's question.

"Had that bat made especial for him by a man in Kentucky. A Falls City original that is. What they call a Louisville Slugger."

"No. I mean, yes, that bat was made by a man in Louisville, but it was given to my pa during the war. It wasn't made for King Kelly."

The man shrugged his shoulders. "It was King Kelly's bat. I can authenticate it as such. He came into this shop himself right before closing last night and sold it to me."

Arnold felt like his heart had been ripped out of his chest.

"You looking to sell that glove?" the man asked. "Might be able to give you a dollar or two for it."

Arnold looked down at the glove in his hand. He had almost forgotten he carried it. The glove he had traded for his father's bat, without meaning to. The glove his hero King Kelly had given him. Arnold went to the front window to look again at the bat on display. He could reach out and touch it, but it wasn't his father's bat anymore. Arnold had lost it. He'd given it away and King Kelly had sold it.

"Said he needed train fare out of town," the man behind

the counter said, as if he could read Arnold's thoughts. He went back to tinkering with the watch. "Some opportunity in Boston. You suppose that means he'll be back with the Beaneaters next season?"

"No," Arnold said, pushing his way outside. "Mike Kelly is all washed up."

Fourth Inning: The Way Things Are Now

Coney Island, New York, 1908

1

Walter wandered the grand boardwalk along the yard outside the Brighton Beach Hotel while his parents checked in. It was early spring, just before the start of the baseball season, and the salty air from the roaring surf was still cool and crisp, like a last gasp before the long hot summer to come. A few brave souls were even wading in the ocean, their navy blue two-piece suits dark against the bright white of the sandy beach.

Walter heard a familiar *crack* and a cheer. Farther down the boardwalk, part of the yard that separated the hotel from the ocean was parceled off into a baseball field, and he rushed to watch. As the batboy for the Superbas, Walter saw more baseball games than probably any other boy in Brooklyn, but the sound of a bat hitting a ball still excited him.

There was a small but enthusiastic crowd of hotel guests watching the game—gentlemen dressed in suits and hats, and ladies wearing extravagant summer dresses, all lounging on reclining beach chairs under umbrellas while colored waiters served them drinks and treats. This was where New York's well-to-do vacationed, and the baseball game was being played for them, and them only.

And it was being played by Negroes.

The runner on second base danced back and forth trying to rattle the pitcher, waving his arms and making silly sounds that made the hotel guests titter with laughter. The pitcher wheeled and pretended to throw the ball to the second baseman, who made believe he'd caught it. The runner played along, getting into a rundown between second and third as the fielders tossed a phantom ball back and forth between them, trying to tag him out. The ladies and gentlemen roared with laughter.

This isn't baseball, thought Walter. *It's a minstrel show.*

The runner slid safely into third base and the invisible ball was thrown back to the big pitcher, who focused again on the batter. The pickoff and rundown might have been fake, but there was nothing phantom about his next pitch, except that the batter had no way of hitting it. It was a blur of motion, a momentary vision that made you think a baseball had been thrown, but you weren't quite sure. Until the umpire called it a strike. The ball was tossed back to the pitcher—there it was, made of real laces and leather, proving that something had actually been thrown—and then he did it again, and again, the batter taking a pathetic, halting swing at the last one before being rung up on strikes.

The players changed sides.

"Who are they?" Walter asked.

"Waiters," said a gentleman lounging next to him. "Some of the hotel staff."

"Cubans," his lady friend said. "Up here for the season. They only play for fun."

The last three pitches didn't look like somebody playing for fun, Walter thought, but he kept it to himself.

"Hey, nice hat," said a boy behind him. Walter turned. Three boys around his age had come up to him. The oldest one might have been thirteen.

Walter touched the Brooklyn Superbas hat he wore. "Thanks. I'm the batboy for the Superbas."

"No," said the big kid. "I mean, 'Nice hat, sheeny. I think I'll take it.'"

Walter clenched his fists. "What did you just call me?"

"You heard me, kike," the kid said.

"I'm not a Jew!" said Walter. It wasn't the first time he'd been called a Jew, and not the first time he'd gotten into a fight over it.

"Sure you're not, Bergstein. With that nose you've got, your mom must have doinked a rabbi."

Walter launched himself at the big one, fists flailing. It was a fair fight for about two seconds. He got in one good blow before the kid and his two friends ganged up on him and beat the stuffing out of him. It would have been smarter to try to break away and run, or even curl up on the ground

107

in a little ball, but Walter clawed and fought, getting himself bloodier in the process.

"Cheese it. Pinkertons!" one of the boys said, and suddenly they were gone. And so was Walter's Superbas hat, the official hat he'd been given with his batboy uniform. He tried to sink to his knees, but a hotel security man pulled him up roughly by the arm.

"All right, we don't stand for any roughhousing here at the Brighton," the man said, his accent thick with Irish.

"I didn't start nothing," Walter said.

The Pinkerton man eyed him. "I'll bet. I know your kind."

"Walter!" his father called. His parents rushed up to him. "Walter, we've been looking everywhere for you."

"Walter, what happened to your face?" his mother asked. "And your clothes!"

"Been fighting," the Pinkerton man said. He gave the same appraising eye to Walter's parents as he had to the boy. "You guests?"

"Er, no," said Walter's father. "They're out of rooms."

"The concierge was kind enough to recommend the West Brighton Hotel," Walter's mother said. She licked a handkerchief and wiped at his face with it. Walter squirmed.

"We won't be troubling you anymore," his father said.

The Pinkerton released his prisoner and nodded. "West Brighton's the place for you," he said. "Now move along."

Walter's father dragged him away, sparing him at least the ministrations of his mother.

"What were you thinking, getting into a scrap at the Brighton? Not a week goes by I don't get called into school for your fighting, but on vacation?"

"They jumped me!" Walter protested. "They called me a sheeny!"

"That's enough of that talk," his mother scolded. Walter saw his mother and father exchange a look.

"Why aren't we staying at the Brighton this year?" he asked. "We stayed here last year."

"I told you, they're out of rooms."

"They have a *thousand* rooms," Walter said. "How can they be sold out? It's not even summer. I thought we had a reservation."

"The West Brighton is just as nice," his mother said, and her tone put an end to the conversation. Walter sighed.

✢ ✢ ✢

The West Brighton *was* just as nice, only it was twenty times smaller. Even so, they had plenty of rooms open.

"The name is Snider," Walter's father told the clerk. Walter thought he'd misheard his father. Their name was Schneider, not Snider. But then his father spelled it for the clerk—S-N-I-D-E-R—and that was how they were entered into the hotel register. Walter started to open his mouth, but a nervous shake of the head from his mother cut him off.

A colored porter carried their bags to their hotel room. Along the way, Walter saw something else different about the West Brighton Hotel. There were Jews here. Lots of them. Russian Orthodox Jews with full beards and long curls who'd been flooding into New York the past few years. The Schneiders—now suddenly the Sniders—were silent until the porter deposited them in their room and closed the door behind him.

Walter could barely contain himself. "Why did you tell that man our name is Snider?"

His father sat on the bed and put his head in his hands. "Please, Walter, not now."

"But our name is Schneider, not—"

"Don't you think I know what our name is?" his father erupted.

Walter's mother avoided the argument by unpacking their bags into the bureaus in the room.

"It's those Russian Jews that have been coming over," said Walter's father. "Why can't they be . . . more *American?* If they would just blend in more, not cling to the old ways so much. Didn't President Roosevelt say there should be no more hyphenated Americans?"

Walter began to put it all together.

"You mean they kicked us out because they think we're Jews!?"

"They didn't kick us out," his father told him. "There were no rooms left."

"But we're not even Jewish!" Walter cried.

"I told you—"

"Did you tell them we're not Jews? What made them think that?"

"Walter—"

"You didn't even tell them? You just let them send us away?"

"I'm sure the hotel manager is a good man," his father said. "Put yourself in his shoes. If the other guests don't want us there, he loses business. It makes no sense for him to hurt himself."

"So we get hurt instead?"

"No one's been hurt."

"The West Brighton is just as nice," Walter's mother finally said. "I like it smaller anyway."

Walter shook with anger. "But we're not Jews! Schneider isn't even a Jewish-sounding name!"

"But Felix Schneider was a Jew, and there's no reason to remind anyone. From today our name is Snider. Not Schneider. Understand?"

"What am I supposed to do, go back to school and say 'My name's not Schneider anymore, it's Snider'?"

"There are plenty of people who change their names to fit in," his mother said.

"Sure. When they step off the boat as greenies at Ellis Island! Not a hundred years after they got here!"

"Don't yell at your mother!" his father told him.

"But I don't understand! We stayed there *last* year and nobody said anything!"

"It's just the way things are now," his father said.

"So," his mother said, "what shall we do before lunch? It says here there's croquet and horseshoes on the front lawn."

Walter got up and left the room. He slammed the door behind him, then sprinted the length of the hall and down the stairs before his father could come after him and punish him for it. He didn't want to play horseshoes or croquet or do anything at the West Brighton. He wanted to be back at the real Brighton hotel.

And he wanted his hat back.

2

Walter felt a thousand eyes on him as he walked among the guests at the Brighton Beach Hotel. He was sure every single one of them was staring at him and thinking *Jew*. That he *wasn't* Jewish made it all the more infuriating. He and his family weren't *anything*. They didn't go to temple and they didn't go to church. They weren't Jewish-American, or German-American, or any kind of -American. They were just *American*.

What was it then that made all these people see him as a Jew? It couldn't be his last name, no matter what his father said. Schneider just sounded German, and there were plenty of Christian Germans. He put a hand to his face. Was it his nose? His curly hair? His complexion? Did he have "Jew" written somewhere on him he couldn't see, in some language he couldn't read?

Walter saw a Pinkerton security man strolling down the Brighton Beach boardwalk and scurried off into the long, crowded field at the foot of the hotel. As big as the place was it would be quite a coincidence to run into the same Pinkerton twice, but it didn't hurt to be careful. For all he knew they'd put a sign up in the Pinkerton break room: "Warning: Be on lookout for fighting Jew."

The colored waiters were still at their game, and Walter found a discreet place to sit and watch. There were more antics—coaches goading players into stealing bases, players speaking what sounded like Spanish, trick throws, hidden balls, primitive acrobatics. But mixed in with all the silliness there was some real baseball being played. After two seasons as the batboy for a National League team—even if it was one of the worst National League teams—Walter knew good baseball when he saw it.

The big Cuban pitcher he had seen earlier was the best of the lot. When he and his team weren't clowning around, he would rear back and fire the baseball at his catcher with all the force of a cannon. Walter half expected to hear an explosion and see smoke as the pitcher released the ball, but instead the only sound and sight were the ball smacking the catcher's mitt, and the dust and dirt that *poofed* out of the leather. In all the time he watched, Walter never saw one batter even make contact with a pitch.

What an addition this pitcher would make to the Brooklyn Superbas! Despite their superlative name the team was truly mediocre, finishing fifth in the National League the last two seasons. A pitcher like this could make them instant contenders!

Walter thought about approaching the pitcher after the game, but in the middle of the eighth inning he spied one of the boys who had beaten him up. He didn't have Walter's hat on, but he wasn't with his friends either. Walter stood and rounded the field, careful to keep an eye out for the other boys or the Pinkertons. The boy he stalked was the smallest of the three, probably nine like Walter. Maybe ten. It didn't matter to Walter how old he was—he was about to get the thrashing of his life.

The boy wandered away from the baseball field and Walter followed him down to the beach, where row after row of dressing tents stood unused. When no one else was around, Walter sprinted up behind the boy and shoved him into one of the empty changing rooms.

"Hey, what gives?" the boy cried.

Walter popped him one in the nose before the boy got his bearings, and then the fight was on. The little guy wasn't a good brawler but he was scrappy. It was a nasty bout, with biting and clawing and hair-pulling. Once or twice Walter thought they might go tearing through the canvas of the tiny tent, but he eventually got his knee in the boy's back and the kid's face down in the sand where he could rain down on him with his fists. The boy coughed and sputtered and begged for mercy, but Walter wasn't in a merciful mood.

"Did you just fall off the tater wagon? Huh? Did you? *I'm—not—a—Jew,*" he said, punctuating each of the last words with a blow.

When he'd beaten the fight out of the boy he got up. The boy was breathing hard, but he didn't make a move.

"Tell your pals I'm gunning for them," Walter said. He kicked sand on the boy and ran far away from the Brighton Beach Hotel, in case the boy or his parents set the hotel security after him.

Farther down the boardwalk the blaring carousel tunes and piped music from Coney Island's amusement parks called to him. Screams and laughter came from Steeplechase Park, where people rode mechanical horses around a great railed track, *pings* and *dings* rose from the arcade games, and everywhere barkers called out, trying to get people to drop a dime on their show, their ride, their attraction.

Competing with the barkers were the soul savers, railing against the sins and depravation across the street. The Salvation Army, the American Temperance Society, the Women's Christian Temperance Union, the Templars of Honor and Temperance, the Anti-Saloon League. They camped out on the boardwalk in their sandwich boards and uniforms and hurled warnings and damnation at all who passed.

"Each of these bottles represents crime and corruption!" one of them cried, tossing full bottles of whisky out into the sea. "Alcohol is an abomination, a plague on our cities and our communities and our families!"

Walter bought a hot dog at Feltman's, ate it in four

bites, then headed for Luna Park. For as long as he and his family had been coming to Coney Island, Luna Park had been his favorite amusement park. It was huge, and always packed full of people—at least in the vacation months, which is when Walter always came. He knew the place like the back of his catcher's mitt. All he had to do was look up and find the giant Electric Tower in the middle and he instantly knew where he was in the park. The tower was covered with electric light bulbs and glowed like the sun night and day.

By nightfall Walter had ridden the Virginia Reel, the Helter Skelter, the Whirl of the Whirl, and Shoot the Chutes—Luna Park's feature attraction—twice. For Shoot the Chutes you rode a cable car to the top of a five-story incline, and then boarded what looked like a long metal cigar to slide down into the lagoon below. Walter thought the ride had to go a hundred miles an hour. After his second trip, when his money was running low, he went to one of the theaters to see what the barker advertised as a "baseball movie."

He was disappointed to find that it wasn't a real moving picture show, just one of those gimmicks where they set slides in front of a projection bulb and show them on a big screen. Still, the photographs were funny, and the guy singing at the piano got laughs with a song about a girl named Katie O'Casey, who was mad for baseball. Walter especially liked the chorus:

"Take me out to the ball game,
Take me out with the crowd.
Buy me some peanuts and Cracker Jack,
I don't care if I never get back.
Let me root, root, root for the home team,
If they don't win it's a shame.
For it's one, two, three strikes, you're out
At the old ball game."

From the pictures Walter wondered if the person who took them had ever really *been* out to the old ball game himself, but he liked the song well enough. From the sound of the applause, the rest of the audience liked it too.

Getting up after the show, Walter spied the pitcher from the baseball game at the Brighton Beach Hotel. He and some of his Cuban friends were just leaving from the back of the theater.

"Hey! Hey you—pitcher!" Walter cried, realizing he didn't know the man's name. "Wait!"

The pitcher didn't hear him, or didn't know he was the one being yelled at. Walter worked his way across the theater, but the Cuban and his friends were already gone by the time he got there.

He couldn't find them outside right away either. Walter slipped in and out of the crowd, hopping up and down to see, and finally spotted them going into the men's bathroom.

The *colored* men's bathrooms.

Walter frowned. The men had dark skin, but Cubans weren't "colored." He waited outside, thinking maybe the men didn't know any better. They were, after all, from another country.

A white couple gave Walter a strange look for standing in front of the colored bathrooms and he moved to a nearby bench, his ears burning red. When the Cuban and his friends finally emerged, Walter had to hustle to catch up.

"Hey, uh, Cubans! Wait up!" Walter called.

The men didn't hear him or didn't care. They didn't stop. Walter ran around in front of them.

"Cubans, wait! Stop," Walter said. The men stopped. *Wait, how am I going to talk with these guys?* Walter thought suddenly. *I don't speak Spanish.*

"Wait-o. Me-o Walter-o," he said slow and loud.

The men stared at him openmouthed.

"Me see you play-o base-o ball-o today-o."

One of the men blinked. "I think this boy's brains are scrambled."

"Wait, you speak English?"

"Uh, what language did you think we'd speak?" the pitcher asked. He had a long drawl like Nap Rucker, the Superba pitcher from Georgia.

"Spanish. Aren't you all Cubans?"

The men looked at one another sheepishly. One of them laughed.

"Oh. Right," the pitcher said. "Well, we, uh, we been off the island a long time."

One of the men snorted and turned around so his face was hidden from Walter.

"Great! Even better," Walter told him. "I saw you pitch today. You were amazing!"

The big pitcher smiled. "Hey thanks, kid."

"I mean it. You were better than half the pitchers in the National League."

"More than half," one of the other men said. The others nodded and chimed in their agreement.

"Listen, I'm the batboy for the Brooklyn Superbas. Why don't you come try out? The team gets back tomorrow from playing exhibition games down South. I'm sure I can get Coach Donovan to give you a look, and I can already tell you you're better than anything the Superbas have got. They're the turds of misery."

"Ain't that the truth," one of the Cubans said.

The big pitcher gave Walter a sad smile. "Aw, look kid. That's awful nice of you, but I can't."

"But why not?"

The pitcher looked around at his chums, who were trying not to laugh.

"Look son, I'm sorry to fool you, but that Cuban thing's all an act."

"What?"

"We're Negroes, son. We're colored, see? I'm even part

Comanche, but my black daddy means there ain't no way they gonna let me play ball for no National League team, no matter how good I am."

"But—at the hotel. They said you were Cuban—"

"Nobody really believes that, kid," one of the others said. "All them white folks, they know we're colored. But if the hotel tells them we're Cuban they can *pretend* we're Cuban so they don't have to fess up to watching Negros play ball, see? That way they can all sit there and drink their mint juleps and enjoy a nice afternoon of baseball without having to get all riled up about it."

"That's the stupidest thing I've ever heard!" Walter said.

The Negroes agreed with him.

"Weren't always like that. Time was, right after the war, when a black man and a white man played ball right alongside each other."

"Who was it made the old American Association? Moses Walker?" one of them asked.

"First and last," the pitcher said. "But that was twenty years ago."

"The good old days," said another.

"Why can't it be like that now?" Walter asked.

The big pitcher shrugged. "That's just the way things are now."

Walter was getting tired of people telling him that.

"It's a nice dream, kid, but it's only a dream," the pitcher said. He and his friends moved away.

"Wait, I don't even know your name," Walter called.

"Joe Williams," the pitcher called back. "But you can call me Cyclone."

Walter left Luna Park that night mad at the world. Which was bad news for the second of the three boys who had beat him up that morning. Walter caught him coming out of Steeplechase Park alone and he beat the tar out of him right there on the boardwalk.

3

It felt like the Pinkertons were out in full force the next day at the Brighton Beach Hotel. Walter wondered if the special attention was for him, but even as he thought it he knew he was just being silly. Still, there *had* been a rash of hotel guests getting beat up. He smiled at the thought and ducked behind a trash can to avoid passing a security guard.

Walter had hoped there would be a baseball game on the lawn this morning, but there was a band playing John Philip Sousa music there instead. That meant he was going to have to sneak into the hotel. But he and his family had stayed there last season, back when it was all right to look like a Jew, and he had a good idea of where the dining hall was. There were fewer places to hide in the halls—and fewer avenues of escape—but he had to find Cyclone Joe.

The dining hall was an enormous room with hundreds of long tables and huge chandeliers that sparkled in the late-morning sunlight. Thousands of guests ate brunch, the noise from their chattering like the hubbub at a ballpark.

In between the tables, dozens of colored waiters moved in a complicated dance, delivering silver platters with the grace of a shortstop catching a ball, sideswiping second, and throwing on to first.

Walter realized someone had come up alongside him and he jumped, worried he'd been copped by a Pinkerton. Instead it was just a colored waiter in a white service jacket.

"Can I help you find your party, young sir?"

"Oh, I'm—I'm not with anyone here. I was actually looking for one of the waiters. Joe Williams. Cyclone."

The colored man blinked in surprise. He looked like he might ask why, but swallowed his question and bid Walter follow him. They went through a set of double doors that led to a long hallway. Farther along, waiters came with empty platters and emerged with full ones.

"You wait right here, young sir, and I'll see if Cyclone is about."

Walter waited for what felt like a long time, and when Cyclone Joe didn't appear he snuck down the hall and peeked in through the round windows on the swinging doors. It was a vast kitchen, hazy with the smoke and steam of food being cooked for five thousand people. Walter pushed his way inside.

One or two of the colored cooks near the door gave him a second glance, but they were too busy to do anything about him being there. The stream of waiters coming in with new food orders was never-ending, and Walter found a place in the corner out of the way of the constant traffic.

Until he saw Cyclone Joe Williams come through the door. Walter jumped out at the big pitcher, who was so startled he juggled his tray. Luckily it was empty.

"Dang, you liked to scare the bejeezus out of me, son! What are you doing here?"

"I got you a tryout, Cyclone! I wired the manager of the Superbas on my parents' hotel account and got you a tryout with the team when they get back to Brooklyn this afternoon!"

It seemed like the entire kitchen got quiet all at once. Cooks and waiters all down the line stopped what they were doing and listened in on the conversation. Cyclone swallowed hard, and Walter could feel everyone's eyes on them.

"I told you, kid. They ain't gonna let a Negro pitch the National League."

"They might if they don't know you're colored."

Cyclone shook his head. "Son, they ain't never gonna believe I'm no Cuban."

"Not Cuban," Walter told him. "Indian. You said yourself you're half Comanche, right?"

Cyclone glanced up at the kitchen staff. They were all still watching them.

"There's plenty of Indians that play in the National League," Walter told him. "Bill Phyle, Chief Bender, Zack

Wheat. All we have to do is tell them you're Comanche and you can play!"

Cyclone didn't look sold on it. "I don't know, kid."

"You're light skinned enough," one of the kitchen boys told him. "You might could pull it off."

"Can't hurt to try," said another. "Not like they's gonna lynch you right there in Washington Park."

"Says you," said someone else.

"They can't say no," Walter told him. "The Superbas need you."

"The Brooklyn Cyclone," one of the other kitchen boys said appreciatively.

"All right," Cyclone said. "What time?"

✦ ✦ ✦

Walter left the kitchen on top of the world. That afternoon he would deliver Cyclone Joe Williams to the Brooklyn Superbas—not as Cyclone Joe Williams, of course, but as Joseph Deerskin, Comanche Indian—and be a hero to an entire borough. With Cyclone Joe Williams as the team's ace pitcher, they might even challenge the Chicago Cubs for the National League pennant.

Outside on the lawn a blue baseball cap with a large letter *B* caught Walter's eye. It was his Brooklyn Superbas hat, and it was being worn by the boy who had taken it from him—the big ring leader who had called him a kike. Walter's fists clenched.

126

The lawn was too open, too visible, and worse, the boy was walking with what looked like his parents. But the weekend was almost over. When would Walter have another chance to get his hat back? And how could he show up at Washington Park today without it?

Walter arranged himself on the path to meet the bully and his family face-to-face. The kid saw him coming a few yards away and grinned like Teddy Roosevelt. He thought he was safe next to his parents—not that Walter thought he could take him in a straight fight anyway.

The family walked up to Walter, who blocked their way.

"Oh, hello," the mother said. "Are you a friend of Henry's?"

Henry snorted.

"No," Walter said. "But he's been borrowing my hat."

"This ain't his hat," Henry started to tell his parents. That's when Walter popped him in the nose, while he wasn't looking. Henry's mother let out a tiny scream as blood spurted from the boy's busted nose. Henry clutched at his face, wailing, and Walter snatched the hat off his head before the boy's father could stir himself into action.

"Help! Someone help! That boy just attacked my son!" Walter heard the man cry. He was already off to the races though, and the ladies and gentlemen out for their Sunday walks parted for him rather than try to stop him. At the last moment a Pinkerton man appeared out of the crowd, but Walter slid around him like a runner avoiding a catcher's tag, tumbled another yard or so, and then picked himself back up to run before the detective could lay a hand on him. Laughing, he ran for the train station that would take him north to Park Slope and glory.

✢ ✢ ✢

The reaction to Joseph Deerskin was not what Walter had anticipated. The Brooklyn players made no move to welcome him to the clubhouse, standing stiff and staring at him like he was something poisonous. Old Patsy Donovan, the Superba's Irish manager and sometime right fielder, chomped on his cigar.

"'Joseph Deerskin,' eh?" he said.

"Just wait 'til you see his tommyhawk pitch," Walter said.

Cyclone glanced at him, but Walter focused on the manager. He knew he was the one he had to convince.

"Where'd ye play last season, Deerskin?" Donovan asked.

"The San Antonio Black—" Cyclone said, catching himself. "The San Antonio Broncos, sir."

"San Antonio, eh? Down to Texas? You're a long way from home, laddie."

One of the players gave a short, hard laugh. Donovan looked up at the team as if gauging them.

"I'm sorry. We've no openings at pitcher this season," he said.

"But we need a pitcher," Walter argued. "Last season you brought in *three* new pitchers. How can there not be any room?"

"Look here, lad, I took you on as batboy because you came in here talking about King Kelly—hell, because you even knew who King Kelly *was*. That means a lot to an old Irishman like me, but this . . ."

"Don't worry yourself, Walter," Cyclone said. He nodded to Donovan. "Thank you for your time, sir."

"No, wait! You've got to see him pitch, Mr. Donovan. He'd be the best pitcher in the National League."

Behind him, one of the Superba players coughed.

"We just don't have the money, Walter," Donovan told him. "I'm sorry."

"No, let's see him pitch," one of the players said. Walter turned. It was one of the boys from Georgia. "I want to see this 'tommyhawk.'"

Walter beamed. "You won't be disappointed. I guarantee it."

The team took the field at Washington Park for practice, splitting up to play an intra-squad game. It was a warm spring afternoon, the clouds high in the bright blue sky over the long low grandstand behind home plate.

Cyclone hung back before taking the field.

"They know, Walter. We ain't fooling anybody. I should just go."

"No! They're going to give you a tryout. When they see how good you are they'll have to take you on the team. And you *are* Indian. That's not a lie."

"It ain't the whole truth neither."

"Are we going to see some pitching today, or are you just

gonna stand around jawing with the batboy?" one of the players called from the field.

Walter stepped back from the field and Cyclone took the mound. The broad-shouldered giant worked the ball in his hands, then slipped on his glove and went into his windup.

Fap! The ball smacked into the catcher's mitt as the first batter took a swing and a miss. Walter jumped and clapped, glancing around to see the team's reaction. Their faces were as stony as they were in the clubhouse, and he stopped cheering.

Fap! Another fastball the batter couldn't catch up to. Walter had to keep himself from cheering.

Cyclone kicked his leg for a third pitch and fired, but this time the batter turned his bat down and bunted the fastball into the ground in front of the plate. The catcher sprang from his crouch and pounced on the ball, then threw down to first—and well over the first baseman, who didn't even jump to try and catch it. The ball went into right field, and the runner was on second before the ball made it back in to the pitcher.

"That's a two-base bunt," one of the players said.

Walter didn't understand. That was no hit, it was an error, clear and simple.

Cyclone took a deep breath on the mound and worked the ball over in his hands before pitching again. This time the batter got a piece of it, knocking an easy ground ball down to the shortstop . . . who let it go right between his legs. Walter was furious. It was a play any kid on any street in

Brooklyn could have made with his eyes closed. The runner scored and the hitter was safe at first.

Cyclone struck out the next batter—despite his attempt to bunt—and struck out the next one looking. The following batter popped up into foul territory near Walter. He backed off as the first baseman came over to catch it, then stared openmouthed as the usually sure-handed Superba let it drop. The first baseman stared back like Walter's father when Walter got in trouble at school for fighting. Like he was disappointed.

Suddenly Walter understood what was happening. The Superbas weren't rusty. They were deliberately misplaying the ball behind Cyclone. This was their way of saying they would never play with a colored man on the field.

The Superbas booted, overthrew, and dropped ball after ball, and Cyclone endured seven unearned runs in the two innings he pitched.

"I think we've seen enough," Donovan said, and Cyclone made no complaint. He tipped his hat to the manager and said nothing to Walter as he left the field. There was nothing to say.

Donovan came over to where Walter stood and they watched as the Superbas went on practicing with a new pitcher. Walter couldn't help but notice they didn't make an error.

"I'm sorry, lad," Donovan said. "It never would have worked. Even if the boys took to him, the other teams would just walk off the field."

"He would have been the best pitcher on the whole team, and you know it," Walter said.

Patsy Donovan didn't say anything to that. He didn't have to.

✢ ✢ ✢

Walter stared out the window of the train back to Coney Island without really seeing anything. It felt like there was a cloud in his brain, fogging everything up. At Coney Island he didn't head for the West Brighton Hotel or the Brighton Beach Hotel, but instead walked along the boardwalk with his head down and his hands buried in his pockets. Coney Island flashed and danced, but he wasn't watching. Bands played and preachers scolded, but he wasn't listening. Walter didn't even feel the wind off the water or the wood beneath his feet.

At the end of the pier Walter stood and stared out at the dark ocean, wondering what was at the bottom. When he was little, he had thought there was treasure there, Spanish gold or pirate plunder. Now he thought that maybe there wasn't *anything* down there, that it was a great empty pit of nothingness.

Walter pulled off his beloved Brooklyn Superbas hat and flung the thing as far out into the water as he could. He watched it splash down, then bob, and then sink, settling in with the rest of the trash at the bottom of the great black sea.

Fifth Inning: The Numbers Game

Brooklyn, New York, 1926

1

"Mrs. Radowski! Mrs. Radowski, it's Frankie!"

Frankie knocked again more loudly so Mrs. Radowski could hear her. The old lady's hearing wasn't so good anymore. Mrs. Radowski's place was right next to Frankie's house, so close that on summer nights Frankie could reach out her window and almost touch it. Most nights, summer or not, Frankie could hear Mrs. Radowski singing some low, sad song in Russian—but at least that was better than what came from the Polish house on the other side.

Mrs. Radowski opened the door all the way when she saw who it was.

"Hello, Frances! You would like to come in for a biscuit, yes?"

"Not this afternoon, Mrs. Radowski. I'm working. Do you want any numbers today?"

"Oh! Yes, please."

Mrs. Radowski found her change purse and handed Frankie a quarter.

"Twenty-five cents today?" Mrs. Radowski usually only bet a penny.

"Yes. Today is good. I win today. I feel it. What is winning on twenty-five cents?"

"One hundred and fifty dollars," Frankie told her.

The old lady patted Frankie's baseball cap. "So clever, young Frances. You should go to university."

"You sound like my pop. Same numbers, Mrs. Radowski? Four-zero-six?"

Mrs. Radowski nodded. It was always the same with her—four-zero-six. Her dead husband's birthday. Frankie waved good-bye and knocked at Mr. Nolan's three doors down. Mr. Nolan spent all Saturday in his undershirt and underwear, no matter the temperature. He took a nickel bet on eight-three-five. He was one of Frankie's few regulars who liked to mix things up. The Steins across the street bought five-five-five for a penny, the same amount the McAllisters on the corner spent on three-five-seven. Three-five-seven was one of the popular ones, even though in the two years Frankie'd been running numbers it had never hit.

Frankie finished her street and worked her way up and down the next couple of blocks. When she'd collected all the numbers for her territory she ran up Flatbush Avenue past the big ticker-tape board at Prospect Park Plaza that showed the sports scores, and then over to the blind pig on Sterling where they ran the policy bank. The front entrance was a dry cleaner's, but the service door led to the saloon in the basement.

Frankie rapped three times, waited, then rapped again. The peephole slid open.

Frankie waved. "Heya Amos!"

The door *plinked* and *clanked* as it was unlocked, and Frankie slipped inside.

"Heya Frankie," Amos said, his deep voice booming. Amos was huge—the biggest man Frankie had ever seen, colored or not, but he was a real softy at heart. Amos smiled. "No notes again today?"

Frankie tapped her noggin through her cap. "Got it all right here, Amos."

He shook his head as he bolted the door. "I don't know how you do it, Frankie. Me, I got trouble remembering my telephone exchange."

"Greenwood 3-6420," Frankie told him.

"That's right! But how did you—"

"I heard the barkeep ask for it one day when you were late and they called around looking for you."

Amos shook his head again. "Too smart for your own good, girl. Best get on in to Mr. Jerome. He'll be waiting for you."

The only two customers in the place sat at the bar hunched over their drinks as Frankie passed through the blind pig. She only ever came on afternoons, when the crowds were light. Her pop told her blind pigs were just places to go and have a drink anyway, joints that would have been dive bars before the Anti-Saloon League types had pushed Prohibition through. It was the speakeasies that were supposed to have singing and dancing too. Frankie would love to see that, but she supposed her father would tan her hide for it.

Billy Sparks was running through his numbers with Mr. Jerome when Frankie got to the counting room. She stood in the corner and figured up the combined earned run averages of the Brooklyn Robins pitchers while she waited. Billy always took a while. He had to write everything down, and it took him and Mr. Jerome the better part of half an hour to decipher his pigeon scratch.

When Frankie's turn came she gave Mr. Jerome the numbers and the bets as fast as he could record them. Mr. Jerome never said anything, but Frankie could tell he liked having someone who could give it to him straight, the way the men at the bank liked it when she worked everything out on her father's deposit slips before he got up to the counter.

Frankie was halfway through the numbers when the door opened and Mickey Fist stepped inside. Mickey Fist owned the blind pig and ran the local numbers game. He had a flat nose and a square head, and he looked like a gorilla stuffed into his big monkey suit. Mickey Fist was about the same size as Frankie's father, but all his weight was in his thick shoulders and arms. Frankie heard he got his name by putting his fist through a door and knocking a guy out cold on the other side, and she believed it.

"This the kid?" Mickey Fist asked.

Mr. Jerome nodded. "Keep going, Frankie."

Frankie didn't know if she was in some kind of trouble or not, but she gave the rest of her take to Mr. Jerome as usual while Mickey Fist listened in. When she was finished she handed over the pocketful of money she'd collected and waited while Mr. Jerome did the count. When he was finished he nodded at his boss.

"She ever get one wrong?" Mickey asked.

"Never."

"What's eight times eighteen?" Mickey asked her.

"One forty-four."

"A hundred and fifty-six times seven?"

"One thousand ninety-two."

"Divided by twelve?"

"Ninety-one."

Mickey Fist looked to Mr. Jerome, who was scribbling with his pencil. He looked up and nodded.

The boss looked Frankie up and down.

"How old are you, kid?"

"Eleven."

"You play it straight, a coupla years we could find a place for you in the organization. You like that?"

"Yessir," Frankie said.

Mickey Fist nodded and left. Frankie let out her breath, and Mr. Jerome did the same. He straightened his glasses.

"You did good, Frankie. Real good."

Mr. Jerome paid Frankie her cut and she went back out into the blind pig. Mickey Fist was talking to another man at the bar.

"I'm telling you, I was there," the other man said. He slapped a newspaper down on the counter and pointed to it. "The numbers in the *Times* and the numbers at the park don't match up. I bet the numbers that came up at Belmont. That means I oughta get paid."

Frankie knew immediately what was going on. The numbers game worked like this: The players bet money on three numbers between zero and nine. The numbers used to be pulled out of a hat, but that was too easy to fix and people wouldn't play. Then somebody got the bright idea to use the daily numbers the newspapers published from the local race tracks. Mickey Fist used Belmont Park. The *New York Times* printed the total take from the Win, Place, and Show bets from the Belmont, and Mickey used the last dollar digit in each one to come up with the daily winning number. If the *Times* said the Belmont took $2,597 for Win, $703 for Place, and $49 for Show, the daily numbers were 7-3-9. It was a good system. The players could check their own numbers in the paper, and since there was no way to fix the numbers everybody knew the game was legit.

Except the *New York Times* didn't always list the numbers right. Like today.

"Sorry pal," Mickey was saying. "You know the rules. We use the numbers printed in the *Times*."

"But they're not *right*, I tell you."

"I get what you're saying, friend," Mickey said. He squared his body toward the other man, making it plain just how much bigger he was. "But we only use the numbers in the *Times*." Mickey made a show of straightening the other man's tie. The guy didn't flinch, but he didn't bat Mickey Fist away either. "And what is it they say? 'If it's in the *Times*, it must be true.'"

Mickey nodded to Amos, who escorted the man out. Conversation over.

A clock on the lamppost outside told Frankie she still had an hour before game time, so she wandered through Flatbush looking for her father. She found him on Carroll Street, whistling and twirling his baton, and ran up from behind him and jumped on his back.

"A robber!" he joked. "Help! I'm being mugged!" He swung her around and she tickled him until he deposited her on the steps of a brownstone.

"How do you always know it's me?" she asked.

Her father reset his policeman's cap and tugged at his shirt to make himself look smart again. "Sweetheart, a real bandit'd lay me out cold on the sidewalk, not ride me around like some steeplechase pony." He took a break from his patrol and sat down on the step next to Frankie. "You run your numbers?"

Frankie showed him her haul. Fifty-five cents. Numbers rackets were illegal—just like blind pigs and speakeasies—

but Pop and most of the other cops looked the other way. Frankie knew most of them went to those places to have a drink when they got off duty anyway, her pop included.

Her father reached into his pocket and pulled out another dime.

"Here. So you can have something to eat at the park."

Frankie kissed her father on the cheek. "Thanks, Pop."

"Who they playing today?"

"The Giants."

"Easy win for the Giants then," he said.

"Brooklyn might win!"

"Those bums? They couldn't hit water if they fell out of a boat."

Frankie's father had been a batboy for Brooklyn a long time ago, but he hated them now, and would never tell Frankie why. He had to be the only Giants fan in all of Brooklyn—or at least the only one who was tough enough to admit it.

"You wait and see. The Robins'll win the pennant this year."

"If you like Brooklyn so much, why do you wear that old Giants hat of mine?" he asked, rubbing the cap on her head. She batted him away and fixed her hair under her hat.

"It's mine now. I like it," she said. She stood to go. "Mickey Fist talked to me today. Said I had a future in the organization."

"Your future is in college, not a numbers racket. I'll see to that if I have to work two jobs for the rest of my days. Three jobs."

"No girls go to college, Pop. That's just the way it is."

Her father frowned. "It doesn't have to be."

"I'll see you later, Pop. All right?" Frankie said, heading off.

"Be home by dinner," her father called. "I'm making meat loaf!"

"Okay, Pop!" Frankie yelled back. She was already turning the corner, on her way to Ebbets Field.

2

There were twelve ticket windows at Ebbets Field, twelve turnstiles, and twelve baseball bats and baseball-shaped lights in the chandelier that hung in the rotunda—Frankie counted them. The grandstand stretched all the way down the right field line and most of the way down the left field line, with a view of a few scattered buildings over the center field wall where Montgomery Street and Bedford Avenue came together. The left field wall was 383 feet from home plate, but right field was just 301 feet away, making it perfect for lefty pull hitters like Babe Herman.

The stands were already beginning to fill, even though the Robins weren't playing all that well again this season. It didn't matter to Frankie, and it didn't matter to anybody else either. Brooklyn loved the Robins. They might have been bums, but they were Brooklyn's bums.

The game was about to start, and Frankie didn't bother finding the left field bleacher seat listed on her ticket. Instead she climbed to the upper deck and looked for a good spot.

She liked to see the action from above. The players might be tiny, but at least she could see the game straight on, not from one side or the other.

There was a whole row of seats close to the front that was almost empty, and Frankie slid across and sat down like she belonged there. A man two seats away from her wrote in a notebook resting on his knee. He had big ears and he held his chin out like he was sucking on a cough drop. He looked up at Frankie, then went back to his writing. Frankie started filling out the lineups in her scorebook.

"What paper are you with?" the man asked her.

"What?"

"Are you with the *World Telegraph and Sun*? The *Daily News*?"

Frankie looked at the guy like he was screwy.

"Sorry. You're sitting on Press Row, so I assumed you were with one of New York's esteemed periodicals."

"Oh cripes," said Frankie. "Does that mean I have to move?"

The man smiled. "No. Stay. Please. It'll be nice to have the company for once. My name's John Kieran. I write for the *New York Times*."

"Frankie Snider," she told him. "I write for P.S. 375, but only when they make me."

Kieran laughed. He nodded at Frankie's hat. "I see you're a Giants fan."

"Can't stand 'em."

"But . . . you're wearing a Giants cap."

"Doesn't mean I have to like 'em."

"A girl named Frankie who sits on Press Row but only writes for school, and who wears a Giants cap but is . . . a Brooklyn fan, I take it?"

"Of course."

"Of course," Kieran repeated. "Do I contradict myself?" he said like it meant something. "Very well then, I contradict myself. I am large. I contain multitudes."

"You don't look so big to me," Frankie told him.

"Indeed."

"Who's playing center?" Frankie asked.

"Gus Felix." Kieran turned toward her. "So, if you sneaked up here, did you sneak into the stadium too?"

"Of course not! I do honest work. I get paid."

"Do you now? We've already established that you're not a member of the fourth estate."

"Are you smart or something?" Frankie asked.

Kieran smiled. "Something." The game started on the field below them, but he seemed more interested in talking to Frankie. "Come now. Information, please. What is it you do for a living? Besides go to school, I mean."

"I run numbers."

"Ah. Yes. Very honest work indeed. And do you wager some of your honest pay on those numbers once in a while?"

"*Chuh.* No. The numbers game is a sucker's bet."

"Curiouser and curiouser. How so?"

Frankie sighed. It was getting difficult to keep score and talk at the same time. "Look, do the math. Mickey Fist's numbers game pays six hundred to one. You bet a penny and win, you make six bucks. You bet a dollar, you win six hundred. Sounds good, right? Only nobody hardly ever wins. You gotta pick the right digits, in the right order. That's a one in a thousand chance, see? It's a sucker's bet. And the marks who play, they think they're not suckers because they only bet a penny or a nickel or a dime. But you bet a penny every day for a year, you spend $3.65. You win once every thousand times, that's like once every two and a half years. Two and a half times 3.65 is nine dollars and thirteen cents. You just spent nine dollars to make six."

"It does seem rather ridiculous when you put it like that."

"Yeah, and Mickey Fist is the one laughing his way to the bank. Say a thousand people bet a penny every day. That's three thousand six hundred and fifty dollars a year, which ain't bad. Now let's say he's got one winner every week—which he don't, but let's just say he does. Six dollars a week times fifty-two weeks is three hundred and twelve dollars. Subtract that from his yearly take, and he's made $3,338, free and clear."

The Robins got the third out, and Frankie flipped her scorebook over for the bottom half of the inning.

"Worst thing is," she told Kieran, "the folks who can't afford it are the ones who play all the time. They see that six hundred to one and their eyes light up. And yeah, they win once in a while, but they'd be better off spending that money when they had it the first time. Mrs. Whitt had her electricity turned off last week. The Orvilles have four boys and haven't eaten meat in a month. This old lady that lives next door to us, Mrs. Radowski, her husband is dead and her only boy died in the war in Europe. Pop says she's broke, but she still finds a coin to play the numbers almost every day."

They watched as the Robins got something going with a double and then a single.

"So tell me something," Kieran said. "Why do you run numbers on your street if you know your neighbors can't afford it?"

Frankie shrugged. "It's just a job I'm good at is all. Besides, it's their money, right? I can't tell them what to do with it."

Kieran went back to scribbling in his notebook, then snapped it shut.

"Finished," he said.

"With what?"

"My story about today's game."

Frankie looked down at the field. It was still the first inning, and the Robins had two men on base with only one out.

"But it's only just started."

Kieran crossed his legs, leaned back, and tilted his hat forward on his head.

"They're all pretty much the same," he said. "I go in right

before the paper goes to press and change the one or two things I got wrong."

"You mean, like who won?"

"Well, yes, occasionally there are some inconvenient facts that have to be worked in. Although with the Brooklyn Robins I can say they lost, and I'm not often wrong. 'Hope is the thing with feathers,' Emily Dickinson once wrote, yet Brooklyn's poor Robins proved featherless yet again today at Ebbets Field.' Something like that. You see how easy it is?"

"Yeah, well, you better start rewriting, mister. The Robins have the bases loaded with only one out, and Babe Herman's up to bat."

Kieran leaned forward to watch. "Ah yes, not the best hitter in New York named Babe, but perhaps a close second."

Herman smacked a double to right, and Frankie stood and cheered. Hank DeBerry scored from third, but then things got crazy. Chick Fewster, who was on first when Babe got his hit, rounded second and slid into third. Dazzy Vance, who had been on second, got caught in a run-down trying to score. Meanwhile, Babe Herman, who'd kept his head down the whole time and run as hard as he could, tried to stretch his double into a triple.

And somehow three Brooklyn Robins ended up standing on third base at the same time.

The Giants catcher tagged them all and let the umpires sort it out. Five minutes later, Herman and Fewster were called out. Babe Herman had doubled into a double play.

Frankie looked across at John Kieran, who leaned out over the rail with a huge grin on his face. He caught her looking and laughed.

"Oh, now I'm going to *have* to add that!"

✛ ✛ ✛

None of Frankie's neighbors won the numbers game that day, but that didn't stop them from betting again. Frankie made enough to go back to the ballpark on Sunday, and she kept score from Press Row until John Kieran showed up late in the third.

"You're just in time," Frankie told him. "The Robins have three men on base."

"Oh?" Kieran asked. "Which base?"

"Ha-ha."

Kieran sat down a seat away from Frankie and opened up his notebook.

"Want to know what's happened?" she asked.

He held up a hand. "No need."

"Why do you come if you're not even going to watch?"

"Oh, I watch the games, Frankie. I watch and enjoy. Particularly the Brooklyn Robins. Who wouldn't like a team with names like Chick Fewster, Trolley Line Butler, Rabbit Maranville, Snooks Dowd, Buzz McWeeny. *Buzz McWeeny,* for heaven's sake! And did you know that this ballpark sits in the exact same spot where a pigsty once stood? They called it Pigtown. Priceless."

"Maybe you'd prefer Yankee Stadium then," Frankie told him.

"Oh, it's very fancy. And Lou Gehrig, Tony Lazzeri, Babe Ruth—they hit a great many home runs and win a great many ball games, if you like that sort of thing. But a foolish consistency is the hobgoblin of little minds. I much prefer the capricious Brooklyn Robins. You never know what's going to happen next."

"Then why don't you write about what really happens?"

Kieran searched the high blue sky for an explanation. "It's like—it's like reading a book to review it. Somehow having to break a book down into its parts to critique it sucks all the joy out for me. I greatly prefer to write my story in advance, and then sit back and enjoy the sum total of the afternoon. Besides, the truth is subjective."

Frankie didn't know what that meant. "I like baseball because it's mathematical," she said. "You know, geometry and algebra and stuff."

"I'm vaguely acquainted with the concepts, yes," Kieran said. He wrote another few lines in his notebook.

"A guy gets a hit, it changes his batting average," Frankie said. "He scores a run, it changes the pitcher's ERA. He makes an error? Count it on the board. There's numbers everywhere. Even the positions are numbered."

"You're quite fond of numbers, I take it."

Frankie recorded the last out of the inning in her scorebook. "Numbers are the one true thing in the world."

"That's a rather bold statement," Kieran said. "And I dare say there are a few poets out there who would disagree with you. You don't think numbers can be made to lie? Here. Take today's pitcher, Burleigh Grimes. Besides his wonderfully Dickensian name, Burleigh Grimes sports a 3.71 earned run average."

"Nothing wrong with that."

"Indeed. It's very good. But consider this: He allows roughly the same number of base runners per inning as fellow Robin Jesse Barnes. Yet Master Barnes possesses an ERA of 5.24."

Frankie frowned. "Well, not every guy that gets on base scores."

"My point exactly. So might we consider Burleigh Grimes 'luckier' than Jesse Barnes? If they are, in fact, comparable pitchers in terms of base runners allowed, how else can we reconcile the differences in their earned run averages? To wit, does Burleigh Grimes' far better ERA mean he is a far better pitcher, or just far more lucky?"

"Okay, so ERA is a measure of luck," Frankie told him. "It's still mathematical."

"Sticking to your guns, eh? All right. How about two players with an equal number of home runs—only one of them hit half of his with men on base, and the other hit none with men on base? The numbers say they are equally dangerous, but is that true?"

"That could just be the fault of the guys batting in front

of him. Maybe he'd hit more with men on if his teammates hit better."

Kieran shook his head, but he was smiling. "I see this is going to be a difficult argument to win."

Below them, Brooklyn slugger Babe Herman came to the plate.

"All right, let's take a different tack," Kieran said. "How many home runs has Babe Herman hit this season?"

"Nine."

"And have you seen him hit all nine?"

"Well, no. So what?"

"So what if he really *hasn't* hit nine. How do you know?"

Frankie frowned. "Because other people saw them. Because the papers said so."

"Ah. And 'if it's in the *Times*, it must be true,' correct? Or have you never seen the paper make a mistake?"

"Well, sure. They make mistakes all the time. Just the other day the Belmont take was wrong. That's what Mickey Fist uses for the numbers game, the last three digits of the Win, Place, and Show takes. But there were other people there who saw it, who know what the numbers really were."

"So those numbers—the right ones—those were the ones used for the payout?"

"No. It was the numbers in the papers. Those are the official ones for the game."

"Aha." Kieran nodded and thought for a moment. "So the numbers lied. They cheated someone out of his winnings."

"Nobody cheated, it was just a mistake."

"But someone *could* cheat, couldn't they?" Kieran said, keeping his eyes on the game. "They could, say, change the last three digits to the numbers one, two, and three, in place of whatever they really were."

"I guess, but it's almost impossible," said Frankie. "They'd have to change the numbers on the machines before the papers got printed."

"Of course. And who in the world could do that?" Kieran asked. He snapped his notebook closed. "Well, it's been fascinating talking with you, Frankie, but I think I'll visit the Brooklyn Museum this afternoon. The Robins don't seem to have that certain je ne sais quoi today."

"They're winning," Frankie pointed out.

"Yes. Perhaps that's what's wrong. Well, my story's written regardless." He stood and arranged his hat on his head. "Besides," he said, "I can always go in tonight and change it at the last minute if I need to."

Down on the field, Babe Herman hit his tenth home run of the year.

At least, Frankie *thought* it was his tenth home run of the year. Now she wasn't so sure anymore.

✧ ✧ ✧

The next morning, Frankie read John Kieran's story about yesterday's Brooklyn game. It left out a few things, but everything in it was right. She didn't know if he'd just made a lucky guess or if he had gone in late, like he said, and changed something. After digesting all the box scores on the page, Frankie flipped to the Belmont take to see if any of her players had hit the numbers.

"Jeepers!" she cried.

Her father jumped, dropping the knife full of jam he was about to put on his toast. "What is it? What's wrong?"

Frankie couldn't believe what she was reading.

The last three digits on the Belmont takes were one, two, and three. In that order.

3

Frankie dashed to the newsstand on the corner of Rogers and Fenimore, grabbed a *Daily News,* and flipped to the sports pages at the back.

"Hey, no reading," said the guy behind the counter.

Frankie read anyway, skimming until she got to the Belmont numbers. The last three were not one, two, and three. She slapped the *Daily News* back on the stack and pulled out a *Telegraph.*

"Hey, this ain't no library, kid."

Frankie found the Belmont numbers just as the newsstand keeper rounded on her. Seven, seven, two—just like in the *Daily News.* Just like everywhere, she expected, everywhere except the *New York Times.*

Frankie shoved the newspaper at the stall keeper and took off, hearing him curse at her all the way down the block. She didn't care. She suddenly understood what Kieran was trying to tell her yesterday. He was trying to tell her he could fix the numbers game.

Frankie ran up the steps to Mrs. Radowski's front door and knocked.

"Mrs. Radowski! Mrs. Radowski, it's Frankie!"

The locks and chains clicked and clinked, and the door opened up to the nice old lady who lived next door.

"Hello, Frances. You would like to come in for a biscuit, yes?"

"Um, sure, Mrs. Radowski."

The inside of the old lady's place was dusty and smelled like mothballs. There were little white doilies all over everything too—the tables, the chairs, even the mantel. Frankie looked at the pictures there while Mrs. Radowski went into the kitchen. There was a picture of her husband, mugging for the camera in a picture booth at Coney Island. Next to that there was a picture of her son, in his army uniform. Frankie barely remembered him.

Mrs. Radowski set a tray of cookies on a table by the fireplace. For some reason she called cookies biscuits, but they were real cookies, and good too. She asked if Frankie wanted some milk with them, and Frankie nodded.

"You're here for my numbers, I suppose," she said, and she started to look for her change purse.

Frankie stopped her. "Mrs. Radowski . . . why do you play the numbers? I know you don't have much money."

"Oh, well, I play because I have so little, you know?" She toyed with her necklace. "I think if I win big, maybe I never have to worry about money again, yes?"

"But the odds are terrible," Frankie told her. "How many times have you won in the last year?"

"Well, none," she conceded. "But you have only to win once, yes?"

Frankie thought about laying it all out for her, the way she had for Kieran, but she didn't think Mrs. Radowski would understand. Or care. She was already opening her coin purse.

"Mrs. Radowski, if you won once, would you stop playing?"

"Well, I don't know—"

"If you won big, I mean."

She fiddled with her necklace again.

"Well, if I win, why should I not keep playing?"

Frankie sighed. It was going to be like this no matter who she asked, she was sure.

"Same numbers, then?" she asked. "Four-zero-six?"

Mrs. Radowski nodded and pulled out a penny. Frankie waved it off.

"Let's make it a quarter," she told her. "It's a good day today. I feel it."

Frankie made her rounds, having similar discussions with a few of her favorites on the block, then checked the clock on the jewelry store at Bedford and Linden. They would expect her numbers at the blind pig within the hour, but she had one more person to talk to first.

Frankie found her father walking his beat near the hospital, but she was so tired from running she didn't even try to jump on his back.

"Whoa there, Frankie, what's the matter? Take a deep breath."

Frankie clutched her knees and waited until she stopped panting.

"Is something wrong, Frankie?" her father asked. He lifted her chin so he could see her face.

"No, Pop. I just wanted—I just wanted to see—if you wanted to play the numbers game today."

Her father frowned. "You know I never play the game, Frankie. It's a sucker's bet. You told me so yourself." He leaned down to look her in the eyes. "You're not playing the numbers, are you?"

"No, Pop. Of course not. It's just that today, well . . ." She couldn't decide how to tell him. "Today . . . today would just be a really good day to place a bet."

Her father narrowed his eyes. "Frankie, what have you gotten yourself mixed up in?"

"Nothing I can't handle, Pop."

Her father crossed his arms, looking bigger and tougher than ever, but he didn't say a word. In her head, it was like Frankie could hear the minutes ticking away.

"I'm due at the blind pig any time now," she told him. "I just thought you might want to bet a little something is all."

Her father gave her the eye, then pulled his change purse and counted out two dollars in coins.

"And don't tell 'em it's from your old man."

"I'll break it up three ways. Bet it for Mr. Wesker, Miss

159

Richmond, and the Coopers down the street. They'll never know they won for us. They never play."

"And I don't suppose I need to pick a number then, do I?" her father asked.

Frankie smiled, which only made her father's frown deepen.

"I hope you know what you're doing, Frankie. Mickey Fist is no man to cross."

✤ ✤ ✤

In the back room of the blind pig, Frankie gave Mr. Jerome her bets. He wondered why seven of her players had chosen the same number, but she told him it was the anniversary of the day Mrs. Radowski's husband died and everybody on the street was doing it in his honor.

Mr. Jerome shrugged. "Don't matter to me what excuse they use to give us their money."

Game time was early that afternoon, and Frankie lost no time getting to the ballpark and taking her seat on Press Row. Kieran sometimes didn't arrive until the first or second inning was under way, but she was too nervous to wait, and ran back down to the main concourse. He was nowhere in sight. Frankie ran up and down both sides of the concession area, then stood under the baseball chandelier to watch the crowds pour in. In a few minutes she got anxious and went searching again. What if Kieran had decided to spend the day at the Brooklyn Botanical Gardens and just make up something about the game later?

Frankie was cursing Kieran's name when she caught a glimpse of his long prim face and white fedora hat. He was down on the field by the dugout talking to big Babe Herman, the Robins' notorious slugger.

"Mr. Kieran!" she called. "Mr. Kieran!"

Kieran said his good-byes to Herman and climbed into the stands.

"Believe it or not, Frankie, I was actually *interviewing* someone for once. You know that double Herman hit that turned into a double play? The big lunk actually blames his *bat.* Says it's defective. You'll never guess what he said he's going to do with it—"

"Mr. Kieran, I need to *tell you something.*"

Kieran crossed his arms. "All right. What's so important it couldn't wait for the third inning?"

Frankie looked around at all the people who were listening to their conversation.

"I want you to . . . come buy me a hot dog," she told him.

"I think you have an elevated idea of what writing twenty column inches a day actually pays," Kieran told her, but Frankie grabbed his jacket and pulled him up to a more private spot on the concourse.

"All right, now what is this all about?" he asked.

"I just wanted to tell you," Frankie said. "I sure hope four-zero-six comes up in tomorrow's numbers game. A lot of my players bet on it."

"Oh. Oh yes. I see," Kieran said. "Four-zero-six, you said?" He jotted the number down in his notebook.

"I hope not *too* many of your neighbors chose that number," he said.

"Only the ones who really need it," Frankie said.

Kieran put his notebook away. "Well, I certainly hope the numbers fall their way. Now, you'd better hurry to your seat if you want to see the first pitch."

"You're not coming? What about the game?"

He patted the notebook in his pocket. "Why watch it when I've already written the article? Besides, I have one or two short errands to run." He tipped his hat and winked. "Until tomorrow, Frankie."

✣ ✣ ✣

Frankie was quiet all through dinner. Her father kept looking at her like he wanted to ask her something, but he didn't. Frankie knew one thing for sure—she couldn't keep working for Mickey Fist, not after this. If it worked, if Kieran did his part, then Mickey Fist and Mr. Jerome had to pay out. They had to pay out, or word would get around that they were welchers and no one would play their game anymore. Even so, they'd still see it for a fix, and they were bound to be unhappy about it.

Tomorrow couldn't come soon enough, and by morning Frankie was tired from a fitful night's sleep. She dragged herself out of bed and splashed water on her face before daring to check the paper. Her father wasn't there that morning—he must have had to check in at the precinct early—but he had left the *New York Times* folded to the Belmont numbers under a bowl of grapefruit.

The last three digits were four-zero-six.

Frankie ran her numbers route that morning just in case the whole thing went over without anybody noticing, but she still waited as late as she could to go in. Amos met her at the door, but he wasn't his usual talkative self and he wouldn't meet her eyes when she said hello. Frankie got a tight feeling in the pit of her stomach, but she went on inside anyway. There were one or two men at the bar again today, but Mickey Fist and Mr. Jerome were waiting for her when she got to the counting room.

"Here she is," Mickey Fist said. "Our little girl who's so good with numbers." He leaned against the wall behind the accounting table, his thick arms folded across his chest. Mr. Jerome shot Frankie a look of warning.

"I've got my daily numbers," she said. Her voice came out like a squeak, and Mickey Fist smiled.

"If they're anything like yesterday's numbers, I ain't sure I want them." Mickey pushed himself off the wall and came around behind her.

"I—I don't know what you mean."

"Sure you don't. Seven people on *your* route bet four-zero-six, and that number just happens to be printed in today's *Times*."

"They just got lucky is all—" Frankie started to say.

Mickey Fist leaned in close to her ear. "*Too* lucky, little girl."

"It was the—it was an anniversary," she stammered. "They were just—"

"Save it." Mickey Fist picked up a *Times,* folded almost exactly like her father had folded his, and jabbed at it with a meaty finger. "The numbers ain't even right. I don't know how they did it, but somebody messed with the Belmont take. We ain't paying."

Frankie didn't understand. How could they not pay? What were they going to tell all their customers? She knew she should have said something, but she was too scared of Mickey Fist to argue.

"That just leaves what we're going to do with you," he said. His breath on her neck was warm and smelled like bacon. "I think we'll start with who put you up to it."

There was a knock at the door and Frankie's father burst through wearing his street clothes. She recognized him now—he had been one of the men she saw hunched over the bar on her way in! She almost ran to him, but his eyes told her to stay where she was.

"What is this?" demanded Mickey Fist.

Amos followed in her father's wake. "Sorry, boss. This fella started raising a stink, then he come busting through the door—"

"Leave it," Mickey said. He stood face-to-face with

Frankie's pop. Frankie was right—they were almost the same size, but where her father was all chest, Fist was all arms.

"I've come for the winnings," her father said.

Mickey Fist laughed. "And who are you?"

"Sergeant Walt Snider, NYPD," her father said, flashing his badge. "We've had complaints."

Mickey Fist blew up. "What is this, a shakedown!? I pay good money to keep my operation in the clear. I ain't paying a red cent!"

"You pay to run an honest game, Mickey. You don't pay up, people talk and we get calls. How long do you think we can turn a blind eye to you cheating folks out of their money?"

"Me? Cheat? That little girl there, *she's* the one running a fix."

"This little girl?" Frankie's father said. "You expect me to believe that?"

"She's smart, this one. But somebody else had to help her out. Somebody at the paper—"

Frankie's father got up in Mickey Fist's face. "You gonna let it get around that you run a dishonest game, *and* that an eleven-year-old girl took you to the cleaners?"

Mickey Fist clenched his fists.

"Go ahead, Mickey. Hit me. See how long that police protection lasts when you nail a cop."

Mickey grinned. "So you're in on this too, huh?" He gave them all a few minutes to sweat, then cracked his neck and took a step back.

"Jerome, how much do we owe?"

"Two thousand, nine hundred and ten dollars," he croaked.

Mickey Fist gave Frankie's father one last glare, then marched around and opened a cabinet at the back of the room. It was stacked with bills and bags of coins.

"Give 'em their cut, Jerome, and tell 'em I don't expect to see either of them ever again."

Mickey Fist brushed Frankie's father on the way out, but her pop didn't rise to the bait. Mr. Jerome counted out the cash with shaking hands, even though Frankie could see it hardly made a dent in the stash in the cabinet.

"You could have really made something in the organization," Mr. Jerome told Frankie as he handed over the money.

"She did," her pop said. He collected the money for her and stuffed it in his pockets. "And now she's through."

Frankie's father steered her out the door past Amos, who gave them the slightest of nods before letting them by.

"All under control, huh?" her father asked when they got to the street. Frankie said nothing. After a few blocks Frankie couldn't hold it in any longer and burst into tears. Her father sat on the steps of a brownstone and pulled her into his arms.

"I'm so sorry, Pop," Frankie whispered.

He held her away so she could see the authority in his eyes. "Don't you *ever* do something stupid like that again, you hear me?"

Frankie nodded, and her father wrapped her in his arms again and let her cry it out.

"That money is for you to go to college, and you're going to make it, do you understand me? You're smarter than me, maybe the smartest Snider there ever was, and I'm going to see you do something with it, you understand?"

"Yes, Pop," Frankie said, and she buried her tears in his big broad chest.

After the winnings had been handed out to Mrs. Radowski and the others, Frankie's father put his uniform back on and went to work. Frankie went to the ballpark, where she found John Kieran lounging in the front row of the upper deck with his white hat pulled down over his face.

"You know, I think I can see my house from here," Frankie said.

Kieran tipped his hat up. "You missed the start of the game. Brooklyn's got two men on."

"Oh yeah? Which base?"

Kieran smiled. "I was starting to worry about you."

"Me? I got everything covered. Thanks to my pop. Lost my job, though."

"Ah, more's the pity," he said. Then he snapped his fingers. "Wait a moment. Now that I think of it, I *did* just hear a young person is needed to operate the ticker tape sports board at Times Square. She would have to be good with numbers, though. Are you good with numbers?"

Frankie jumped up and hugged Kieran, then sat down

beside him. They enjoyed their afternoon quietly for a few outs.

"So, did you already write your story?" Frankie asked. "Who's going to win?"

"Brooklyn. Four to two," he said. "Give or take a few runs."

Kieran ordered two hot dogs with everything from a vendor, and Frankie watched him pull out a wad of bills to pay for it.

She whistled. "Look who's Mr. Rockefeller now."

"Well Frankie, it just so happens I got very lucky in today's numbers game . . ."

Sixth Inning: Notes of a Star to Be

Fort Wayne, Indiana, 1945

1

The reaction to Kat when she walked into the visitors' locker room was not exactly what she had hoped for. She had come right from the Fort Wayne train station and she was still wearing the clothes she'd left Brooklyn in: her best dress and a pair of her mother's real spiked heels. The only thing she carried was her mother's tattered old scorebook, which she clutched with both hands like a life preserver. Everything else was in her suitcase, including her glove.

The other girls stopped changing into their uniforms and stared. Kat gave a little wave and heard someone snort.

Ms. Hunter, the team chaperone, cleared her throat. "Everyone, meet the newest Grand Rapids Chick: Katherine Flint from Brooklyn, New York."

"Kat," she corrected. "Everybody calls me Kat."

A couple of the girls laughed, and someone made a little "meow" sound.

An older man in a baseball uniform walked in and the girls suddenly looked busy. Kat figured he must be the manager.

"This the new girl?" he asked.

Kat held out her hand. "Kat. Katherine. Flint," she said, nervous. The manager didn't shake her hand.

"You play infield or outfield?"

"Well, either one, I guess, but—"

"Ziggy's leg is twisted, so you'll play second today. Get suited up," he said, then disappeared into his office again.

Kat ran her hands down the side of her dress, looking for pockets that weren't there. Why had she packed the last of her gum in her suitcase?

A lanky blond girl lacing up her spikes eyeballed Kat and shook her head. "We're gonna lose twenty to nothing."

Kat had tried out for the All-American Girls Professional Ball League last year when she was fourteen, but they told her she was too young. This year they had told her the same thing, but then just after the start of the season she got the call—there were already so many injuries the league was giving her a chance. Could she meet the team in Fort Wayne, Indiana, by the end of the week?

Darn tootin' she could.

Ms. Hunter brought Kat a uniform like the rest of the girls wore, a belted dress with a tunic that buttoned up the side. In the middle of the tunic was the round logo of the Grand Rapids Chicks. Kat looked at herself in the mirror. The skirt had no pleat to it, and Kat felt like she was wearing a parachute. Worse, the hemline came down to her knees. She felt a little corny putting on a skirt to play baseball or softball or whatever it was they were calling the game the girls played. Ever since the war had started, girls everywhere had been wearing pants and dungarees. But Kat wasn't getting paid to design uniforms, she reminded herself, she was getting paid to play baseball. She would have worn a sack cloth if they'd asked her to.

"You'll do great, Katherine," Ms. Hunter told her. "And I've found a glove for you to use in the game."

"I don't suppose there's anyplace I could get a stick of Orbit, is there?" Kat asked. Orbit was her favorite kind of gum.

"Marilyn," Ms. Hunter called. A girl almost the same age as Kat came running over. "Marilyn, can you run to the concession stand and bring back a pack of Orbit gum for Kat?"

Ms. Hunter gave her a nickel and the girl hurried off.

"Thanks," Kat said. She ran her hands down her sides and caught herself again. If she didn't get control she'd be touching wood again soon—and in a dugout with all those bats, that could be a problem.

Kat saw one of the players nudge another and nod at her. "Straight off the train and already she's making demands."

Not a good start, Kat thought.

Before the team took the field, the manager came back to give them a pep talk, such as it was.

"All right girls, listen up. We're awful. The papers say the Chicks can't buy a win, but I'm gonna prove them wrong. You beat the Fort Wayne Daisies today and I'll give each of you a five-dollar bill. Including Ms. Hunter."

That was the sum total of his speech.

Kat marched up the staircase with the other girls into the bright sunshine of an Indiana afternoon. She was blinded at first, but when she finally was able to look around she saw . . . people. Hundreds, maybe *thousands* of people! As many as might be at a Brooklyn Dodgers game. The stands all up and down the first and third base lines were packed and the fans cheered as the team stepped onto the field.

Kat spun where she stood and laughed. For a moment her laughing was the only sound she could hear, the crowd and the band and the loudspeakers fading into the background like someone had turned down the volume on the wireless of her life. She couldn't remember the last time she'd felt the sun so warm on her skin, or laughed so hard, or felt so alive. She was a million miles away from her father's war letters, her mother's ten-hour-a-day job, Hattie's victory garden. For the first time in years she wasn't worried about blackouts or scrap drives or food rations. Kat was a Grand Rapids Chick—a professional baseball player!—and she wanted this feeling to last forever.

When Kat came back to her senses she was the only one left on the field. The Chicks were already in their dugout, and they stared at her like she was a void coupon. Kat quickly dipped down under the awning and started touching the ends of baseball bats sticking out of a box.

"Looks like they're recruiting from the nuthouse now," the tall blond girl said. Embarrassed as she was, Kat couldn't stop—until Marilyn the bat girl came running up with a pack of Orbit. Kat almost kissed her.

"Thank you thank you thank you," she said, ripping the pack open and popping a stick in her mouth. She immediately felt better, and the urge to touch the bats was gone.

Every last one of the girls in the dugout stared at her like she was crazy.

"*V* for victory time, girls!" Ms. Hunter called. "*V* for victory."

Kat was confused, but she followed the other girls out onto the field where they formed a V shape with the girl at the point standing on home plate. A *V* for victory in the war against Germany and Japan, Kat guessed. She ran to the last place on the end of one of the letter's arms just as the band began to warble "The Star-Spangled Banner."

When the anthem was over Kat ran to second base by way of first. Touching the bag was one of her rituals, and to break it would mean she'd lay an egg for sure. That didn't make the look from the girl at first base any easier to swallow, though.

No, Kat thought, definitely *not a good start*.

Kat held her own at second, handling three chances in the first two innings just fine. In the meantime, she liked watching the pitcher, the tall blond girl who'd said the Chicks were going to lose with Kat in the lineup. She had a big windmill windup, and she'd swing her long arm in a circle a few times before slinging the ball at the plate. *Pow!* The ball would pop in with such force that Kat didn't know how anybody could hit it.

Luckily she didn't have to, and the Daisies pitcher wasn't nearly so crafty. When Kat came up to bat in the third the pitcher laid a fat one right across the plate that Kat laced to right for a hit. She got another single in the fifth and a double in the seventh and scored both times. But neither time was she met at the plate by her teammates, and they gave her the silent treatment in the dugout like they didn't want her there. Kat took a seat at the far end of the bench, away from all the players, and touched the end of every bat in the box.

Thanks to Kat the Chicks won the game—their first in six tries, she found out later—and the manager made good on his promise of five bucks each to the girls. Even so, none of the girls would speak to her, and on the bus ride back to their hotel she was the only girl to sit by herself. As she peered out the window at the passing streetlights, Kat wondered if coming here had been a terrible mistake. The team didn't want her, and if they didn't want her, well, she could just go home to Brooklyn . . . But the thought of going back to that life, that world, almost brought her to tears.

Just when she thought things couldn't get any worse, Ms. Hunter told her she'd be rooming with Connie Wisniewski, the tall blond pitcher who'd made fun of her in the dugout. Kat waited for the rest of the girls to pull their luggage out of the bottom of the bus and hauled her own bag into the hotel by herself. She eyed a couch in the lobby and wondered if she'd be sleeping there tonight.

Kat found her room and put the key in the lock, half expecting the bolt to be latched. It was unlocked, but that was just the first of the surprises. The entire team was crammed into her room, and they cheered for her as Connie Wisniewski swept her up in a hug.

"What? But, I don't—" Kat tried to say.

"I'm so sorry for being snippy," Connie said. "You just looked so small and dolled up when Ms. Hunter brought you from the station, and we haven't won in so long."

Girls clapped Kat on the back and introduced themselves, laughing about how hard it was to keep giving her the cold shoulder while she single-handedly won the game for them.

"It was all my idea, I'm afraid," Connie told her. "Consider this your initiation."

Ms. Hunter came by and shooed the other girls off to their own rooms.

Kat gasped. "My mother's scorebook! I gave it to Ms. Hunter before the game!"

Connie caught her at the door. "Calm down, calm down." Connie pulled the scorebook from her satchel and handed it to Kat. "I wondered when you'd notice."

Kat wiped tears from her eyes. "If I had lost this—it's got every game me and my mother have ever seen in it, all the old Brooklyn Robins games she went to as a kid."

"Yeah, well, there was one missing, so I added it at the end."

Kat flipped through to the last used page. It was today's game—the Grand Rapids Chicks versus the Fort Wayne Daisies. Kat hugged Connie.

"The first of many, kid. You're gonna be here a long time, Kat. I know it."

Connie peeked out the door down the hall, then flipped open her suitcase and pulled out a pair of pants.

"Come on. Get dressed."

"Get dressed? For what? It's after curfew."

Connie went to the window and slid it open. "We're sneaking out to a party."

"What, are we going to climb out the window like monkeys?" Kat asked.

Connie looked back, one leg already over the sill.

"Of course not. How many monkeys do you think have ever climbed down a hotel fire escape?"

✦ ✦ ✦

The party was in a cemetery. The Fort Wayne catcher lived in her own place beside a graveyard, and that was where she threw shindigs when visiting players came to town.

Kat touched trees as they made their way deeper among the tombstones.

"Don't get spooked," Connie told her. "We haven't once been loud enough to raise the dead."

Not that they weren't trying, Kat thought. Someone had brought a portable phonograph player, and Frank Sinatra was crooning "Saturday Night (Is the Loneliest Night of the Week)" with a backup chorus of Daisies bobbysoxers. The rest of the girls sat on gravestones sipping beers and smoking cigarettes.

"Hi-de-ho!" a woman called, and she hopped down to give Connie a hug. Connie introduced her as Pepper Paire, the star catcher for the Fort Wayne Daisies.

Kat ogled the cemetery and the broad, bright sky full of stars. "I can't believe I'm here," she said.

"In a cemetery?" Pepper asked.

"In a cemetery, in Fort Wayne, in Indiana, in the league."

"First day," Connie explained.

"Ah," said Pepper. She smiled. "Yeah. You know, back home during the Depression, I used to play on this little softball team sponsored by the local grocery. If we won, we each got to go back to the store and fill up a bag with as much stuff as we could cram into it. Now I get paid a hundred dollars a week."

"More'n my pa ever earned in a week, that's for sure," Connie said.

Pepper raised her bottle. "Pennies from heaven," she said.

"Where are you from?" Kat asked Pepper.

"Los Angeles."

Kat moved closer to her, making sure not to step on any graves. "What's it like? California, I mean. I've only heard stories."

"It's always sunny in Los Angeles," Pepper said. "Sunny and warm. Not like here. And there's movie stars all over. You see 'em in the drugstores, in diners, walking along on the streets. There's professional softball leagues for girls too. They pay you if you're good enough. Not like this, but enough to make a living."

"I always wanted to play ball for a living," Kat said.

Pepper smiled. "Who doesn't, kid? Who doesn't?"

There was an argument over what would be played next on the phonograph. Eventually the Bing Crosby fans won out and the graveyard was serenaded by "Swinging on a Star." Kat stared up at the constellations. She'd never seen so many stars in the sky, not from New York, where lights burned night and day.

"I don't think she heard you," Connie said.

Kat blinked. "What?" Had someone asked her a question?

"She looks like she has a lot on her mind," Pepper said. "She needs to talk to Mrs. Murphy."

Pepper beckoned for Kat to follow her, and they walked alone to a quiet part of the cemetery. The catcher stopped in front of a small, simple gravestone that said only: "Hope Murphy."

"Kat, meet Mrs. Murphy," said Pepper. She brushed the top of the stone like she was cleaning it. "How you been, Mrs. Murphy? I've been on a road trip, so I haven't had a chance to drop by and say hello."

Kat looked around, wondering if this was another initiation.

"I come out here sometimes and talk to Mrs. Murphy," Pepper said. "I tell her all my deepest, darkest secrets."

"Who is she? I mean, did you know her?"

Pepper shook her head. "Just another gal like us. All she ever did and was, all that's left is her name." Pepper put a hand on Kat's shoulder. "You tell Mrs. Murphy whatever it is you've got on your mind. She'll listen. She's good at that."

Pepper left Kat alone at the grave. Kat looked around, sure a gang of players was waiting to jump out and laugh at her the minute she started talking to the stone.

"Um, hi," Kat said. "I um, I don't . . ." She looked around again. There wasn't anywhere Pepper or the other girls could be hiding, and the party carried on behind her. "I guess I do have something to say. Something I've never told anybody. I don't—I don't want the war to end. I want my dad back safe of course, but I wouldn't be here, now, without the war. There wouldn't even *be* a girls' league. And my mom, she's so smart, so good with numbers, but she only got a job as an engineer because all the men are off fighting. And Hattie, she's smart too, and she could go to school, get a good job if she wanted. The whole world's different now because of the war, and I know that there's less food and things to go around, and everybody's working so hard, and people are dying, but—"

Kat closed her eyes, ashamed of what she was saying. "I wish it could be like this forever."

Kat backed away from Mrs. Murphy and tripped on another stone. She hadn't realized she was standing on someone else's grave.

2

Coach Meyer moved Kat up a couple of places in the lineup at home against the Rockford Peaches. She came to bat in the second with two girls on and no outs, and took time to do her pre-hitting ritual: Touch both ends of the bat, touch both toes, and draw an *H* in the sand, for "hit."

"You gonna hit sometime before the war ends, rookie?" the catcher asked.

Kat nodded to the umpire that she was ready and the pitcher went into her windup. The first pitch was a hanging curveball, and Kat sent it high and deep to right, where it banged off the wall of a lock factory for a home run. The crowd went dizzy. Connie, who was coaching first base that day, cheered Kat as she ran the bases, and the Chicks poured out of the dugout to celebrate with her when she reached home plate.

"You put one in orbit!"

"Like her gum!"

"You're the cat's meow, Kat!"

"She's a killer!"

"Killer Kat!"

Kat tried to get back to the dugout, but Alma Ziegler wouldn't let her.

"You gotta run the gauntlet," she told Kat. Was this some new initiation? A girl pointed Kat toward the first base line, where Kat saw Grand Rapids fans beckoning to her. Still not sure what she was in for, she ran over and found that every one of them wanted to shake her hand or clap her on the back.

The Chicks won their second game in a row, and the girls took Kat out on the town for dinner and then loaded up on the bus again for the next day's game in Kenosha against the Comets. Kat stuck with Connie, and together they sat mesmerized for a moment by the passing streetlights outside their window.

"Round and round the lake we go, where we stop, nobody knows," Connie whispered. "I probably been around Lake Michigan more times than Chief Pontiac."

"Have you been in the league a long time?" Kat asked.

"Just since last season. I came in with the Chicks when they were in Milwaukee. We won the whole thing, but nobody came out to see us. Same thing happened to the Millerettes in Minneapolis. But Grand Rapids has been great, same as Kenosha, Racine, Rockford, and the rest. Good crowds, good people."

"One of the fans today," Kat said, "when I went over to 'run the gauntlet'? One of them slipped me a dollar bill!"

Connie laughed. "I know! They do that sometimes. Teeny Petras made fifty dollars that way last season! Sent every bit of it back to her mother in Jersey."

"I also—I also got this." She handed Connie a slip of paper with a man's name and telephone exchange written on it.

"Ohhhh, no." Connie wadded the paper up and tossed it back over her head. "You're too young for that sort of thing. Looks like I'm gonna have to stick to you like glue, kid. Keep you away from Grand Rapids' more *sinister* element."

Kat smiled. She knew Connie was only kidding about the sinister element, but she was glad to have a friend. She was glad for so many things right now, and immediately felt guilty for it. She took a paper gum wrapper out of her pocket to fold it into little squares.

"So what's with you and the gum and the bats?" Connie asked.

"The bats?"

"Touching all the bats in the dugout."

Kat blushed. "I—I sometimes get nervous and have to touch all the wood I can see." She reached over and touched the wood frame of the bus window.

"You loony or something?"

"It wasn't always this bad, but once my dad got drafted—"

"Europe or the Pacific?"

"Europe. He's fighting in France." Kat unfolded the little wrapper and took a cigar box with a bear on the cover from her bag. The box had been her father's once. Inside, there were two cigars and a framed photo of him in his army uniform. Underneath that there was a stack of Orbit wrappers, all folded and unfolded again, one for each day he'd been gone. Kat added the new wrapper to the stack and touched all four corners of the wooden frame.

"I've never missed a night," Kat said of her little ritual. "It's stupid, but I like to think it keeps him safe."

"I'm sure it does, Kat."

Kat took a deep breath and stared out the window. The city streets of Grand Rapids had turned into the rolling farmlands of Michigan. She wanted her father to come home safe, wanted the Allies to beat Hitler, wanted her family to stop scrimping and saving and eating nothing but potatoes and carrots from their victory garden. But out here, in the vast flatlands of the Midwest, she was already starting to forget about all that.

And the forgetting felt good.

A murmur of laughter came from the poker game at the back of the bus, and Kat turned in her seat. It was late and she knew she should be sleeping, but she didn't want to miss a thing. It had been like this last night, and the night before, and Kat wondered if she would ever want to go to sleep again.

A broad, dark shape made its way down the aisle and stopped beside them.

"Katherine, are you awake?" It was Ms. Hunter, the chaperone.

"Yes, ma'am. I'm sorry."

"No need to be sorry, dear." Kat could practically hear the chaperone smiling in the dark. "I'm sure you're excited. Things have been such a whirlwind that I didn't have time to give you your beauty kit."

Connie snorted. Ms. Hunter put a booklet in Kat's lap, and in the occasional glow from the passing streetlights she could read the cover: "A Guide for All-American Girls: How to Look Better, Feel Better, Be More Popular, by Mme. Rubenstein."

"It's hard to walk in high heels when you've got a charley horse," Connie told Kat.

"You don't have to read it now," Ms. Hunter said, "but the league wants you to read it soon, and to always be as attractive and healthy and charming as possible."

"And play to win," Connie added.

"Of course," said Ms. Hunter. "And play to win."

Kat flipped through the packet, dismayed that she had homework to do.

"There are really only a few important things to remember," Ms. Hunter said, like she could read Kat's mind. "Always wear a skirt and look your best. Don't get your hair cut short, and never wear Oxfords or masculine-looking shoes. And the biggie: No fraternizing with opposing players."

"No what?"

"You're not supposed to be chummy with the girls on the other teams," Connie translated. "They don't want the league to look like a sorority."

"That's it," Ms. Hunter said.

"But last night we—"

Connie elbowed Kat, who quickly shut up.

"I'm sure Connie or one of the other girls can steer you clear until you get into the swing of things, but if you have any questions, do come to me, all right, dear?"

"All right, Ms. Hunter."

Kat flipped through her beauty manual again and saw that the last page was blank but for a headline: "Notes of a Star to Be." She liked that. "A Star to Be." It reminded her of Hollywood and all of Pepper Paire's stories of California. Kat looked out the window, trying to see the stars, but she couldn't see past her own reflection.

"So where'd you learn to hit like that?" Connie asked.

"Hmm? Oh, back in Brooklyn. I practically grew up at Ebbets Field, and there was always a stickball game going on around the neighborhood. I just played with the boys, learned to hit whatever they could throw. My whole family's mad for baseball. No time for that now, though. Dad's off in France, mom's an engineer building battleships, and Hattie, that's my sister, she runs the house."

And I ran away to play games.

Connie caught Kat thinking. "You miss them? Your family?"

Kat looked at her face in the window.

"No. Is that bad?"

Connie shrugged. "Some go one way, some go the other."

A car beside the bus started honking and flashing its lights. The girls craned forward to see what was going on as the bus slowed down and pulled over. There was some discussion between the bus driver and whoever it was who had flagged them down, and soon he came back with an armful of soda crates.

"Local Coca-Cola fella says he wants to donate a few cases to the team!" the driver announced. The girls hooted and hollered, and some of them leaned out the window to thank their benefactor and blow him kisses as he unloaded more from his trunk. Each girl took a bottle as they got passed back, and more cases were stacked into the front seat of the bus before it pulled back out onto the road.

"I tell you, this is the life!" Connie said.

Kat couldn't agree more. She tapped the top of her bottle three times before popping it, and Connie looked at her suspiciously.

"Keeps the fizz down?" Kat tried.

"Uh-huh." Connie clicked bottles with her and they drank.

The pit stop for Cokes had riled the girls up again, and Alma Ziegler—the girl Kat had been playing for while she was hurt—crab-walked her way forward from seat to seat. At the front of the bus Alma turned her jacket inside out and put her cap on backward to the calls and whistles of the team.

"My fellow All-Americans, let us pray," she said.

The girls were still buzzing, and half of them were laughing uncontrollably.

"I said let us pray, you creeps! Now shut it!"

There were stifled snorts throughout the bus, but everyone got quiet.

"My friends, many games hath we strayed from the winning path."

"Amen, sister!" Connie cried out. There were more laughs.

"And long have we toiled under Meyer, who God knows ain't no Moses."

"Aw, shut it and let me get some sleep," the manager called from the front of the bus. He was met with raspberries.

"And lo, Saint Feller and Saint DiMaggio and Saint Williams and the rest have left and gone to war."

Connie and the other girls put their caps over their hearts, and Kat hurried to do the same.

"In short, dear sisters, it is high time for a Sermon on the Mound."

The girls pelted Ziegler with their caps, and she very un-preacherly shot one of them back at a girl. In a moment she had her eyes closed and her hands raised in mock prayer again.

"Is there a rookie in this house of worship tonight?" she asked.

There was more whooping from the back of the bus, and Kat felt her ears begin to redden.

"I said, is there a rookie among us tonight!? Come forth, rookie, and be saved!"

"I thought I already had my initiation," Kat whispered.

"You did," said Connie. "This is different. This is a baptism."

Connie nudged Kat into the aisle and the team cheered. Not knowing what to do, Kat staggered down the aisle of the still-moving bus and stood before Ziegler. The veteran put her hand on Kat's cap and then pushed her to her knees.

"What is thy name, rookie?"

"Kat. Katherine Flint."

"Kat Katherine," Zeigler said, getting laughs, "you come today to the church of women's baseball from Hoboken, New Jersey."

"No, Brooklyn, New Y—"

"Don't interrupt me, sister. You come to us from Hoboken—or wherever—and offer yourself to this most holy of games. Do you give of yourself freely and clearly to baseball?"

"I do."

"Do you accept the central tenets of our faith—the run, the hit, and the error?" she said, then quieter, "But not so much the error."

"I do."

"Are you in body, mind, and spirit—particularly body—truly *in the game?*"

"I am!"

"And when my leg gets better, are you going to play some other position so I can have my old job back?"

Kat laughed. "Yes!"

"Good. Now that that's out of the way—are you going to get a hit tomorrow, sister?"

"Yes!"

"Are you gonna play your little rookie heart out tomorrow, sister?"

"Yes!"

"Let me hear it!"

"Yes, sister!"

"Then let it be known to all here who bear witness, that from this day forth you shall be known as 'Killer Kat' from Brooklyn—not Hoboken—and that you are, fully and truly, a Grand Rapids Chick. I now baptize you in the name of Tinker, and of Evers, and of the holy Chance."

Ziegler lifted Kat's cap, and she felt something rain down on her head. Too late she realized it was a bottle of Coca-Cola. Kat jumped up, sputtering.

Alma Ziegler laughed. "Say hallelujah, sisters!"

The bus rang out with hallelujahs. Kat pushed the sticky wet hair out of her face and smiled.

"Hallelujah," she whispered.

3

"We ain't got forever, you know," the catcher told Kat as she went through her hitting routine again.

Kat grinned at her as she stepped into the batter's box. "Hallelujah, sister," she said, getting a strange look from the catcher. It didn't matter. Nothing anybody else thought or did mattered. Kat was a Grand Rapids Chick, and nobody could take that away from her. She pounded the fourth pitch she saw into right center, and Connie, coaching first base again, windmilled her toward second. Without looking Kat knew the throw was coming in, that the play would be close, and she slid feet first into the bag.

"Safe!" cried the umpire.

Kat popped up. "Hallelujah!" she told the umpire, almost laughing.

"Hallelujah!" Connie echoed at first, hopping up and down. The Chicks had won five straight games, and Kat had climbed higher and higher in the lineup.

Kat was so happy she almost didn't feel the sting, but

then it came on like an electric burner heating up. Her exposed leg beneath her skirt was all scraped up from her slide, like she'd slid on concrete. It hurt like all get out, but Kat fought back the tears. It didn't matter. Nothing else mattered. She was a Grand Rapids Chick.

And the town of Grand Rapids loved Kat almost as much as she loved it. Cars honked and people waved as the girls made their way down the street. Restaurant managers gave them the best seats in the house. Strangers sent them drinks. Little girls asked for autographs. Kat couldn't imagine a better life, and the page in her guidebook, "Notes of a Star to Be," quickly filled with her memories and her hopes and her dreams.

But there was one dream Kat had she did not want, a dream that came to her again and again, night after night, a dream that would not stop until she tore herself from sleep, panting and sweating. In Kat's dream, she was tapping on the ends of bats. She knew it was a dream, because there were hundreds of thousands of bats, more than she could ever count, but she could never rest until she had touched them all.

But tonight as Kat touched the bats her tapping grew louder and louder, until it was a knocking, a pounding . . .

Kat woke with a start to someone knocking on the door of the hotel room she shared with Connie.

"Wake up, girls!" Ms. Hunter called through the door. "Wake up!"

Kat's vision was fuzzy, but she could see she still wore the clothes she had worn out last night when Connie had taken her to meet some friends on the Racine Belles. She pulled the covers up to her chin, afraid Ms. Hunter might come inside. The knocking was more insistent, and Connie worked her pillow over her head.

"Go away," she moaned. "It can't be afternoon. We just went to sleep."

"It's victory in Europe!" Ms. Hunter called through the door. "It's over! The war in Europe is over!"

Kat shot straight up in bed. Connie did the same. The knocking stopped and they heard Ms. Hunter banging on the next door down the hall.

"What did she say?"

"She said the war in Europe is over," Kat said, still dazed.

Kat heard clapping and cheering out on the street, and Connie rushed to the window.

"Jeepers, look at 'em!" Connie marveled.

The street was alive with people. It was like the indoors was too small to hold their happiness, like they had to get outside before their joy blew out all the doors and windows. People were crying and singing and dancing and hugging. Down the hall, some of the other girls were tearing up toilet paper and shoving it out the window like confetti. Church bells rang across the city, and car horns joined in the hullabaloo.

"Let's go down!" Connie said. She grabbed Kat's hand and pulled her out the door but stopped when she could feel Kat holding back and turned to see her tears.

"Kat, what is it?"

"I'm happy. I am," Kat blubbered. Her tears spilled out like boiling water. "It's just, I just got here and all and—"

"Oh, Kat," Connie said. "Are you worried about the league?" Connie pulled Kat into a hug. "You batty kid! This isn't the end—it's just the beginning!" Connie held her out at arm's length. "The league is stronger than ever! We're not going away just because Hitler's been squashed. Why, someday your own daughter will be playing for the Chicks. I guarantee it. And think of your pop! He's safe now. You won't have to be collecting those gum wrappers and tapping on wood anymore."

Kat gasped. "My Orbit wrapper!" She pulled an empty wrapper out of her pocket. "I forgot to put it in with the others when we got home last night!"

"But see? It doesn't matter!" Connie told her. "It's victory in Europe!" Connie whooped and dragged Kat with her down the steps. On the sidewalk, a man Kat had never met before picked her up and kissed her. The lady behind him gave Kat a bear hug, and little children ran among the revelers waving American flags and flying little toy airplanes. Kat looked around for Connie, but she had already disappeared into the crowd.

Maybe Kat was wrong. Maybe the league would go on. Maybe this life would go on, long after the war was over. Maybe forever. Maybe people had seen the way things could be and would never go back. She wiped her eyes again, and suddenly thought what a disappointment Mme. Rubenstein would find her right now—just out of bed, clothes rumpled, hair a mess, eyes red and puffy from crying. Kat started to laugh, and soon she couldn't stop. It hurt to laugh, but it was a good kind of hurt, like pulling a splinter.

Farther down the street there was a fountain, and anybody who wouldn't jump in was being thrown in. Connie was dancing on the edge, and Kat jumped up and took her in with her, crashing into the cold pool, cackling all the way.

Their game that night was canceled. Everything was canceled, and for one glorious night, all of America took the break it *hadn't* taken ever since the attack on Pearl Harbor more than three years ago. But in the morning it was back to business as usual. There was still victory in the Pacific to work for, and it wasn't going to be won playing in fountains and dancing in the street. Still, everywhere Kat went that day there was a smile on people's faces, and when she got to the ballpark she learned it had been sold out for hours.

Kat gave Marilyn a nickel for a pack of Orbit and the bat girl dashed off as the players began to get changed. Meyer posted the lineups, and Kat, Grand Rapids' newest star, was batting third. Connie gave Kat a punch in the arm to congratulate her as Marilyn ran up to them.

"That's fast," Kat said. "Back already? Somebody get this girl a contract!"

But Marilyn wasn't back with Kat's gum. She was back

with a Western Union telegram. It was from Kat's sister, Hattie, back in Brooklyn.

"It's probably to tell me we won," Kat said. "Like I wouldn't hear."

Connie frowned and sat on the bench beside Kat to read over her shoulder. Kat tore into the envelope and read the thing through.

"Oh my God, Kat—"

Kat read it through again.

And again.

It was a short message. All it said was:

"Father killed in action May 8. Body buried in France. Mom says stay and play."

Connie hugged her. "Oh, Kat. I'm so sorry."

"It's not true," Kat said. "May eighth. That's V-E Day. That's the day the war ended. How could he die on May eighth? This isn't right." Tears fell even as she said it. She knew it was right, knew her sister would never have played such a terrible joke, never written unless she was absolutely sure. She knew it was true because she had not put the gum wrapper in the cigar box that night. She hadn't touched her father's picture frame to keep him safe. She knew it was her fault her father was dead.

"My fault," she sobbed.

"No, Kat. No," Connie said, rocking her.

Kat found her glove through her tears and stood to join the other girls on the field. Connie caught her hand.

"Let me tell Ms. Hunter and Meyer," Connie said. "They'll understand you can't play today."

"No. Please. I have to play today. I have to play today, because tomorrow I have to go home."

"What? No. Why? What good would that do?"

"I have to be there for my mother. Help Hattie—"

"If your mother is designing battleships, I don't think she needs much help. And besides, look, she even told you to stay."

Kat sobbed. She hadn't missed her family before, but now she did. Now she wanted to bury herself in her mother's arms and cry like a baby.

"There's a time and a place for everything, Kat, and this is your time. Your place. You're a star."

"*V* for victory, girls!" Ms. Hunter called. "Come on. Let's go."

Kat wiped her face with her glove, and Connie let her go. Kat walked up the steps and out onto the field to take her place in the V. She knew the sun was shining and the flags were waving and the crowd was cheering, but to her the world was a different place. To her it was still and quiet, and *she* was the only one moving, her weeping the only noise.

The national anthem played, and Kat cried. She cried for her father, she cried for her mother, she cried for Hattie. But most of all she cried for herself, because she knew Connie was right. She knew she was going to stay.

Seventh Inning: Duck and Cover

Brooklyn, New York, 1957

1

There was a trick to flipping baseball cards. Just the right flick of the wrist, just the right release, just the right spin so that it fluttered and floated to the ground and landed heads-up on the picture side or tails-up on the stats side. There was a knack to it, an art, and Jimmy Flint was the undisputed card-flipping king of PS 161.

"You gonna flip sometime this century, Clyde?" Eric said.

Eric Kirkpatrick was the biggest, ugliest kid in the fifth grade. Legend had it he'd been held back not once, but twice. He was also just about the only Yankees fan in the whole neighborhood, probably just because everybody else was a Dodgers fan. But Jimmy didn't care about any of that right now. Jimmy had taken three straight cards from him, and now Eric's beloved Yogi Berra card was facedown on the playground cement. All Jimmy had to do was land his next card faceup beside it and both cards would both be his.

"Stay back! Give him room!" Jimmy's friend Ralph said,

pushing away the small circle of watchers their game had attracted.

Jimmy drew the next card from his stack—Jim Gilliam, second baseman for the Dodgers. Jim Gilliam was just about his favorite baseball player of all time, the Brooklyn Dodger who'd taken over at second base for Jackie Robinson when Jackie moved to the outfield. Jimmy had a special fondness for second base; his mother had played second for the Grand Rapids Chicks back when there was a women's league, and Jimmy himself had spent the last three months of one of those seasons at second base, growing inside her. He figured if ever there was a born second baseman, he was it.

"Come on, already! Recess is about to end!"

Jimmy kissed his card, took a moment to get the angle just right, and flicked it. Time slowed as it fluttered end over end, then settled to the ground. It was faceup. He'd won!

The boys around them erupted, cheering and clapping him on the back. Jimmy added both the cards to his stack and his friend Ralph raised Jimmy's hand like he was a winning prizefighter.

"Ladies and gentlemen—the undisputed winner and cham*peen*, Jimmy Flint!"

"Gimme that back," Eric said.

"What?"

"Gimme that card back. You cheated."

"Cheated how?" Ralph demanded. "He won fair and square!"

"Back off, monkey boy," Eric said.

Jimmy's black friend took a step back with the rest of the crowd, and Jimmy couldn't blame them. He was right in Eric's sights, though, and there was nowhere for him to run.

"Bet you come from a long line of cheaters, don't you, Skinflint? Bet your dad was a cheater. But—oh, that's right, you don't know who your dad is, do you?"

Jimmy clenched his fists, but he knew he would never take a swing. Eric would wipe the pavement with him. The circle of boys hid them too well for him to call for help too; Jimmy couldn't see Mrs. Holloway at all.

Eric stepped closer. "Come to think of it, I haven't seen your mom around the neighborhood in a while either. She off looking for your dad?"

Eric's friends snickered.

"My mom's in California. She's a scout for the Dodgers!"

"You sure about that, Skinflint?" Eric flicked a finger at the Keep the Dodgers pin on Jimmy's jacket. "Or did she finally skip town for good like your stupid ball team?"

"Get bent!" Jimmy said, then immediately wished he hadn't.

"What's that?" Eric said. "Did I just hear you tell me to get bent?"

The class bell rang, and Mrs. Holloway called for everyone to come inside. Eric Kirkpatrick shoved Jimmy and he fell, losing his stack of cards and scraping his hands on the cement. Eric kicked the loose cards around with his sneaker and took back all of the ones he'd lost, including the Yogi Berra card.

"You're the one who's going to get bent, Skinflint," Eric said. "After school."

"Skinflint's going to get bent!" one of Eric's goons repeated as they walked away.

✤ ✤ ✤

Back in the classroom Jimmy sulked at his desk. The rest of the class was buzzing because Mrs. Holloway had turned on the radio. The only other time Jimmy could remember listening to the radio in class was two years ago, when Johnny Podres had twirled a shutout to beat the Yankees in game seven of the 1955 World Series. It was the only World Series the Dodgers had ever won—and the way things were going, the only World Series they would *ever* win. At least for Brooklyn.

But this time their teacher tuned in to hear a very different enemy, one far scarier to Jimmy than the dreaded Yankees:

Sputnik. The first man-made spacecraft, built and launched by the Russians.

It was everywhere on the radio, on every station. The Russians had beaten the Americans into space.

"It's a satellite," Mrs. Holloway explained. She drew a crude picture of the Earth on the blackboard, then drew a circle around it, punctuated by a small white dot. "It circles the Earth like our moon does, only much faster and much closer."

"It looks like a baseball Duke Snider hit into orbit," Ralph said. That got some laughs, but Jimmy wasn't in the mood.

"Wait—" the NBC announcer said. "Our observers tell us Sputnik is just now passing over the Eastern Seaboard!"

Half of Jimmy's class left their desks and rushed to the windows to look for it, but Mrs. Holloway waved the students back to their seats. "Sit down. Sit down. You won't be able to see it right now. You'll have to wait until sundown, and you'll probably need binoculars or a telescope."

They might not be able to see it, but they could hear it. The radio played the signal live as it passed overhead, a speck in the sky.

Beep, beep, beep, beep, beep, beep, beeeeeeep, beep, beep, beep—

It was monotonous. Endless. Inhuman. Jimmy got goose bumps.

Ralph leaned forward to whisper in Jimmy's ear. "Man, that's creepy."

"What—what does it mean?" Betsy Walker asked.

"It means the Commies can drop atomic bombs on us from space!" Eric said from across the room. Mrs. Holloway's fifth-grade room exploded into chatter and she tried to calm them down again.

"Children, children! Please, calm down." Mrs. Holloway shot Eric an exasperated look. "The Russians are not going to drop atomic bombs on us from space, or anywhere else.

Because they know if they do, we'll drop atomic bombs right back on them."

"But then we'll *all* be dead!" Betsy Walker wailed.

"Yes, and no one wants that, now, do they?" Mrs. Holloway said.

The radio announcer signaled that the station was going to a commercial, with more Sputnik news to come. "And later, of course, more of our ongoing coverage of the crisis in Little Rock, Arkansas, where federal troops—"

Mrs. Holloway switched off the radio. "Enough of that. You'll have nightmares enough as it is. Please open your arithmetic books." The students moaned, but did as they were told.

Jimmy still heard the *beep, beep, beeeeeeep* of Sputnik in his head, but if he couldn't figure some way to sneak out after school the Russians didn't matter: Eric Kirkpatrick was going to kill him first. While he was supposed to be working on long division Jimmy calculated the many ways Eric could devise to bring him down. When he was supposed to be learning about adjectives in English class, Jimmy outlined how Eric could modify his face. In music he noted that Eric could beat him like a wood block; in science he experimented with the hypothesis that Eric would dissect him. By the time social studies came around at the end of the school day, Jimmy was convinced he would end up stuffed in a locker like a mummy in a sarcophagus.

Which gave him an idea.

✤ ✤ ✤

That afternoon Jimmy stood in darkness, straining to hear the slightest sound in the hallway. School had been out for almost an hour, and in the silence all he could hear was the echo of Sputnik's robotic laugh in his head: *beep, beep, beep, beeeeeeep—beep, beep, beep, beeeeeeep—*

A door handle *ka-chunked* somewhere down the hall, and Jimmy held his breath. Eric couldn't have hung around this long looking for him, could he? Jimmy closed his eyes and said a silent prayer as a pair of sneakers squeaked down the hall, closer and closer and closer, until they stopped just outside his locker.

"Psst. Hey, Jimmy. You still in there, man? The coast is clear."

"You sure?" Jimmy whispered.

"I followed them all the way to the soda shop. They're gone, man."

Jimmy torqued his shoulder around to reach the latch and opened his locker.

Ralph shook his head at him. "Man, I can't believe you stuffed yourself in your own locker."

"Better than getting pounded by Eric Kirkpatrick," Jimmy said when he had worked his way out. "Now I just sneak down the back stairs and—"

The doors down the hallway *ka-chunked*, and Jimmy froze.

"You sure they didn't follow you back?" Jimmy whispered.

"Yeah. Positive," Ralph said.

Multiple sneakers squeaked their way closer.

"Um, pretty sure?" Ralph amended.

"Run!" Jimmy said, and the moment they took off they heard the other sneakers pick up the pace. Jimmy and Ralph dashed out the back doors, leaped down the flight of stairs to the sidewalk, and flew down Crown Street. A quick glance back over his shoulder told Jimmy all he needed to know— Eric and his gang were after them.

"Split up!" he cried when they hit the corner of Nostrand Avenue. Ralph took a right and Jimmy took a left toward Montgomery and Ebbets Field. At Ludlam Place Jimmy ducked down the bottom steps of a brownstone and hid, knowing he couldn't outrun the gang forever. He did his best to fade into the stone wall of the stairwell as they ran past, and it seemed to work. He waited until they had turned the corner down the street just to be sure, then doubled back.

As he ran home, Jimmy kept one eye on the sidewalks and one eye on the skies. He couldn't decide which was worse: Eric Kirkpatrick or the Russians.

2

Jimmy got to school early the next morning, hoping to avoid meeting Eric and his friends. Between Sputnik and Eric Kirkpatrick, Jimmy hadn't even been able to sleep. Nobody was in the hallway, and the clock on the wall told him class wouldn't start for another hour, but it was worth the wait. He put his book bag in his locker and went inside Mrs. Holloway's room to practice his card flipping, secure in the thought that he had at least delayed his beating until the first recess of the day.

He was in his seat talking with Ralph about *The Adventures of Rin Tin Tin* on television when Eric Kirkpatrick came into class, right before the bell. Eric watched Jimmy the whole way to his seat, and Jimmy knew he'd only made things worse by playing keep-away. As bad as it sounded, maybe he should just have let Eric and his gang beat him up yesterday, or come to school on time and let them catch him in the hall. Then again, maybe if he stayed away from Eric long enough he'd just give up.

Across the room, Eric popped his knuckles and grinned at Jimmy.

Or maybe not.

The bell rang and Mrs. Holloway began setting up the film screen. Yesterday the radio, today the projector—it was shaping up to be an interesting week. Usually Jimmy was as excited as the other students in the class to have a film, not so much because they liked films, but because they could close their eyes and pretend to be watching while they napped. Today, though, Jimmy was too focused on self-preservation.

"Today's film is called *Duck and Cover*," Mrs. Holloway said, "and what with all the talk about Sputnik and the Russians, the principal thought we should start showing it again. This film should answer a lot of the questions you had yesterday about an atomic attack. Alice, if you would please get the lights?"

The lights went off, and the classroom resounded with the fake farting noise their pants and skirts made when they all slouched down in their seats at the same time. A girl in the back corner giggled.

"Pay attention, please," Mrs. Holloway said.

The film began with a cartoon turtle in a helmet walking down a path, enjoying a nice spring day. His name was Bert the Turtle, a song told them. Behind Jimmy, Ralph snickered. If he hadn't been so wound up, Jimmy would have too. This was kids' stuff.

Suddenly a monkey dangling from a tree hung a firecracker in the turtle's face. Bert ducked into his shell. The firecracker exploded.

"Bad monkey!" Ralph said, and the class laughed. Mrs. Holloway shushed them again.

When the smoke cleared, the tree and the monkey were gone. But Bert the Turtle, the narrator told them, was safe because he had ducked and covered.

The film then showed a classroom not unlike Jimmy's, where the teacher was showing them how to duck under their desks and cover their heads when an atomic bomb exploded.

"We all know the atomic bomb is very dangerous," the narrator told them. "Since it may be used against us, we must get ready for it, just as we are ready for many other dangers that are around us all the time."

"Yeah, like Eric Kirkpatrick," Ralph whispered.

Jimmy didn't know how Ralph could joke around right now. All he could think about as he watched was Sputnik circling overhead. *Beep, beep, beep, beep, beep*—

"You will know when it comes," the narrator said. "There is a bright flash, brighter than the sun, brighter than anything you've ever seen." The film went white, and then cartoon houses and trees were knocked down and thrown around. This was what Sputnik could do: Drop a bomb that would blow up his house, his block, his school, Ebbets Field—*everything*. Kill his mom, his grandmother, his great-grandfather. Him.

There were two kinds of attacks, they were told—with warning and *without* warning. When there was a warning, they would hear air raid sirens, and must get to shelters as quickly as possible. "But sometimes the bomb might explode without any warning!" the narrator said. When they saw a flash, they were supposed to duck and cover, no matter where they were. The film showed pictures of students in the cafeteria, boys riding bikes, children playing on playgrounds. They showed families having picnics, people sitting in buses, men driving tractors. Each time the flash came and the people ducked and covered. But if an atomic bomb could knock down buildings and destroy his neighborhood, Jimmy wondered, what would it do to people?

Bert the Turtle came back at the end. "Remember what to do, friends. Now tell me right out loud—what are you supposed to do when you see the flash?"

Some kids in the film answered back, "Duck and cover!" but none of Jimmy's classmates said a word. The movie ended, and the loose end of the film *slap-slap-slapped* against the empty reel. Mrs. Holloway switched off the film projector and turned on the lights.

"What are you supposed to do?" Mrs. Holloway asked. "Let's hear it."

"Duck and cover," Jimmy answered with the class.

"Right. Let's practice. Ready? Just like in the film. There's a *flash!* Quickly, down under your desks."

Jimmy and his classmates slid out of their seats and crawled under their desks. Most of them, at least.

"Eric, get down under your desk," Mrs. Holloway said.

"I ain't afraid of no atomic bomb. This is sissy stuff."

"Don't be silly. Now duck and cover."

Jimmy watched as Eric slid out of his desk and crouched, not really ducking or covering. For his part, Jimmy wasn't going to play around. He pulled himself as tightly into a ball as he could and shielded his neck and head with his hands.

"Good, Jimmy. Good, Ralph. Cover your neck better, Betsy," Mrs. Holloway said, going up and down the rows.

"Man, this is what you ought to do when Eric Kirkpatrick comes after you," Ralph whispered. "Duck and cover."

Jimmy knew his friend was kidding, but right now he wasn't as worried about Eric as he was about the atomic bomb. All he could hear in his head was Sputnik flying overhead.

Beep, beep, beep, beep, beep, beep, beeeeeeep—

✤ ✤ ✤

Just because he was afraid of the atomic bomb didn't mean Jimmy was eager to get beat up. At the first recess of the day he avoided Eric by telling Mrs. Holloway he wasn't feeling well and asking to stay inside. He *wasn't* feeling well, not after the film, but it was really just a ploy to buy himself a little more time. Like the Russians, Eric Kirkpatrick could attack at any time, and if Jimmy couldn't really duck and cover to avoid him, at least he could hide out in his turtle shell a little while longer. He skipped the other two recesses of the day the same way, which amused Eric and his friends to no end.

"What's the matter, Skinflint? You scared of something?" Eric asked on the way outside. Jimmy just kept his head down, silently plotting a way to escape that afternoon without being caught.

Ralph stayed with Jimmy after school while he did everything he could think of to delay leaving the classroom. He volunteered to beat the erasers, wash the blackboard, even sweep up.

"Man, what you gonna do now?" Ralph asked him when he was finished.

"I don't know. Do you think they'd let me spend the night?" he joked.

"You want me to go check out in the hall, see if they're there?"

Jimmy checked the clock. "No. There's a Keep the Dodgers rally at Ebbets Field I wanted to go to anyway. Maybe if I can slip past them I can lose them again on the way."

"Man, you are one brave dude," Ralph told him.

Jimmy stepped into the hall, expecting to see Eric and his friends right away—but they weren't there. He glanced up and down the hallway. They had to be lying in wait for him somewhere.

"Where are they?" Ralph asked.

Jimmy went to his locker, half afraid Eric was hiding inside, waiting for him. He wasn't, of course, but that just meant he was waiting to jump him somewhere else. Jimmy collected his books and headed for the front stairs. Eric and his friends weren't in the stairwell, but when he reached the bottom step Jimmy froze. Through the bank of doors that led outside to the front steps of the school, he could see Eric Kirkpatrick waiting for him. Suddenly his bravado ran out.

"I—I'm gonna go out the back way."

"Yeah. Sounds like a good idea to me," Ralph said. Together they jogged up the stairs and down the hall to the back stairs. Jimmy was just about to push his way outside and make for home when he saw two of Eric's gang hanging out on the back steps. He ducked back inside.

"They covered both the exits!" Ralph whispered. "Man, they must really want to get you bad. What are you gonna do now?"

Jimmy retreated into the stairwell—and noticed for the first time that the stairs kept going down beyond the ground floor.

"Hey, where do these stairs go?"

Ralph shrugged. "Basement, I guess."

Jimmy jogged down the first flight of stairs to the turn.

"Can you see me from up there?"

"No."

"All right," Jimmy said, coming back up. "I've got an idea."

❖ ❖ ❖

Ralph burst through the back doors and almost made it past Eric's buddies before they grabbed him.

"Whoa there, monkey boy. Where you going in such a hurry?"

"Yeah, and where's your little friend?"

"Eric got him. Coming out the front door."

"Swell," one of the boys said.

"Please, no—leave him alone."

"Heh. Some hero you are," the other boy said. He shoved Ralph against the wall and headed for the door. "Come on," he told his friend. "I don't want to miss the fun."

Ralph gave Eric's friends time to go inside and climb the stairs, then pulled the door open and whistled softly. Jimmy came running up the stairs from the darkness below and slipped outside. Together the two friends ran as far as Nostrand Avenue before they stopped to say their good-byes.

"I owe you one," Jimmy said.

"Great. How about you give me your Jim Gilliam card, then?"

"What!? No way!"

"Gil Hodges, then."

"Deal." They shook on it, and Ralph took off for their street while Jimmy headed for Ebbets Field.

There was a small group of people assembled at the corner

of Sullivan and McKeever when Jimmy got there. Some of them wore sandwich boards with slogans on them and sang songs trying to convince the Dodgers to stay in Brooklyn. A woman wearing a "Keep the Dodgers" pin and a Brooklyn cap sat behind a little table nearby, and Jimmy gave her the pages of signatures he'd collected for the petition to get the Dodgers to stay. The woman added them to an impressive-looking stack on a clipboard and offered Jimmy a pin, but he told her he already had one.

A man with a bullhorn led the crowd in a Dodger fight song, and Jimmy sang along as loud as he could. But even as he sang, Jimmy couldn't help but wonder who heard them, or who was actually going to read the petition. The season was over. The Milwaukee Braves were playing the New York Yankees for the World Series, and his mother and the rest of the Dodgers' front office were already in California getting ready for next season. It suddenly felt silly to work so hard to keep the Dodgers in Brooklyn when they clearly didn't want to stay, and Jimmy slipped away before the song was even finished.

Jimmy shuffled up the steps to his great-grandfather's house and went inside. Great-Grandpa Snider was watching television, and Jimmy plopped down beside him. They watched in silence until Jimmy's grandmother appeared in the doorway to the kitchen.

"I thought I heard someone come in. Did you have a good day at school, Jimmy?"

"Yes ma'am."

Grandma Frankie waited like there was something more.

"Your teacher called. Mrs. Holloway. She said you didn't go out for recess at all today. Said you seemed all mopey."

Jimmy stared at the ground.

"You're not getting sick, are you?"

"No ma'am."

"So what about it, then? Why won't you go out to play?"

"I just—I just needed some time to work on my Keep the Dodgers petition," Jimmy lied.

"Oh, Jimmy. You know that man never meant to keep the Dodgers here. He was just looking for a reason to leave."

"I know."

"Dinner'll be ready in a half an hour," she told them, disappearing into the kitchen.

Jimmy couldn't bring himself to get up, so he sat and watched *What's My Secret?* with his great-grandfather. They put the new contestant's secret up on the screen so the viewers at home would know what the panel was supposed to guess. It said: "Every time Sputnik goes over my house my garage door opens."

"What's his name?" Great-Grandpa Snider said out of nowhere.

"Whose name?"

"The boy who's giving you trouble on the playground."

Jimmy flushed and clammed up. His great-grandfather looked away from the TV at him.

"I don't know any red-blooded American boy who doesn't want to go outside for recess. You're not a Commie, are you?"

Jimmy laughed and Great-Grandpa Snider smiled.

"No, sir. And his name is Eric Kirkpatrick."

"Bigger'n you? Ugly cuss?"

"You know him?"

Great-Grandpa Snider laughed. "I've known a lot of him over the years. So what are you going to do about it?"

"Duck and cover," Jimmy said.

His great-grandfather harrumphed. "So that's the plan? You're gonna run away all your life?"

Jimmy shrugged. "At least until junior high."

"I tell you," Great-Grandpa Snider said, "you better do something about it now, or you're going to be ducking and covering your whole life. That's what my pa did, and it wore him down."

"But what can I do?"

"Fight back. If he's bigger'n you, step on his toes. Then, when he's hopping around cussing, pop him one in the nose."

Jimmy didn't know what to say. He'd never heard his great-grandfather talk like this.

"Better yet, shoot him a knee to the groin. Don't matter how big a man is, that'll take him down every time. No matter what you do, you find a way to fight back, or you'll be a victim all your life."

"Y—yessir," Jimmy said, sliding off the couch. "Thanks."

Jimmy went out back into their small yard. It was almost twilight, and he lay down on his back to see if he could spot Sputnik flying overhead. Next door, the Ramirezes' radio was tuned in to the news, where the broadcaster was talking about "Mutually Assured Destruction." Then they replayed that *sound*, the sound of Sputnik drawing a bead on them from orbit: *Beep, beep, beep, beep, beep, beep, beeeeeeep, beep, beep, beep—*

The Russians were in space, the Dodgers were going to California, and Eric Kirkpatrick was going to pound him to a pulp.

Other than that, his life was perfect.

3

Jimmy watched the second hand ticking away on the clock above the chalkboard in Mrs. Holloway's classroom. *Tick, tick, tick*—it beat with the haunting regularity of Sputnik. But Sputnik was death that could come without warning, and Jimmy's more immediate concern was the death that was coming *with* warning: Eric Kirkpatrick, who had come over to Jimmy's desk that morning to tell him in no uncertain terms that there would be no escape this afternoon.

Tick, tick, tick—skipping recesses and lunch, Jimmy had five hours and twenty-three minutes left until the end of the day, and maybe the end of his life.

When it was time for math Jimmy and the rest of the students pulled out their arithmetic books, but the teacher told them they wouldn't be using those books anymore. They had ordered new math textbooks, books about geometry and algebra, and the students would begin using them within the week. They would be getting new science textbooks too.

"This is math you would be learning later, in junior high,

but the school board has decided to step things up a bit. I'm sure you'll all do fine," Mrs. Holloway said. She gave them all an encouraging smile. "Instead of your usual math work today, we're going to watch a film to help prepare you for what's to come. Can someone fetch the film projector for me? Jimmy?"

Jimmy jumped. He'd been staring at the clock and not really paying attention.

"And who will go with him?" Mrs. Holloway asked.

"Ooh! Ooh! Me!" Eric Kirkpatrick said, waving his hand frantically in the air.

"Why, Eric. I've never known you to be so . . . enthusiastic about helping," Mrs. Holloway said. "You and Jimmy then. Off you go."

Jimmy couldn't move. He knew exactly why Eric had volunteered to go with him to get the projector. This time he was going to get Jimmy before he had another chance to slip away.

"Remember—duck and cover!" Ralph whispered from behind him.

Jimmy rose like a condemned man and met Eric at the door. Eric beamed at him.

"Back in a flash," Eric told Mrs. Holloway, and he opened the door for Jimmy with mock politeness.

Jimmy walked alongside Eric down the hallway, wondering when the attack would come. Not here, he realized, not around the other classrooms. Eric would wait until they were alone together in the A/V room.

He could just run away, but to where? If he ran back to class he'd be a laughingstock. If he ran home his grandma would just send him right back. He could run off to the movie theater, spend the day there in the dark, and then head home after school was over, but then what about tomorrow? And the day after that? And the day after that? No, Great-Grandpa Snider was right: To run now would mean he'd be running away all his life. He'd have to *move* to get away from Eric Kirkpatrick, and that wasn't going to happen.

But fighting him wasn't going to happen either. Great-Grandpa Snider might have been able to stand up to bullies, but Jimmy couldn't. He'd never been in a real fight in his entire life, and he was sure if he started this one—or even fought back—it would only make things worse on him.

Jimmy was beginning to think that maybe duck and cover was the best option after all.

Eric pushed him inside the A/V room and closed the door behind them. The place was filled with film projectors on carts and reel-to-reel tape machines, and had the metal/plastic smell of the future. Oddly, Jimmy wondered if this is what Sputnik smelled like.

"No running away this time, Skinflint."

Eric knocked him backward into a cart, and while Jimmy was trying to keep himself from falling Eric punched him in the stomach. It was like running into his bike handlebar times a thousand, and Jimmy fell to his knees, groaning.

"You think you're pretty smart, don't you, Skinflint?"

Jimmy kept his eyes on the floor.

"You got nothing wise to say this time? That's what I thought. All right, Clyde. This is how it's gonna go. I'm gonna pound you, but if you say anything about what happened and get me in trouble, we'll just do this again, see? Mrs. Holloway asks, and you tell her you—"

Eric was interrupted by something howling outside—a siren. They both froze.

"What gives?" Eric asked.

Jimmy knew that sound. They'd just heard it the day before in class.

"It's a civil defense siren!"

Eric ran to the window. "I—I see it! I see a bomb!"

"Duck and cover!"

Jimmy and Eric dove underneath a strong-looking wooden table, and Jimmy covered his head and neck with his arms.

"You think it's the Russians?"

"Of course it's the Russians, Skinflint! Who else would it be? But did you see a flash? I didn't see a flash. They said there would be a flash!"

Jimmy didn't see anything. He had his eyes shut so tight they made faint radiating patterns against the back of his eyelids. Over the wail of the siren, Jimmy kept hearing the drone of Sputnik. *Beep, beep, beep, beep, beep, beep, beeeeeeep*—

This was it. He would never see his mother again, never see Grandma Frankie or Great-Grandpa Snider again. His house, his school, Ebbets Field—his entire world would be gone.

And then the siren stopped. In the sudden silence, Jimmy could hear their breaths against the cold tile floor.

"You think it's over?" Jimmy asked. "I didn't hear any explosions."

"I don't know—but I ain't getting up until somebody tells me to get up."

The two boys waited under the table, hands over their heads, for what seemed like ages—but Jimmy wasn't going to get up until Eric did. Just when his legs were starting to cramp up, Jimmy heard the door to the A/V room open.

"Oh, boys! I'm so sorry." It was Mrs. Holloway. Jimmy and Eric raised their heads. "The drill is over now. You can come out."

"Drill?" Eric asked.

"We didn't know when it would come, but we announced it to the class when the sirens went off."

"But Eric saw a bomb. He said so."

"Saw a bomb?" Mrs. Holloway said. "I'm not sure you would actually see one falling. Exploding, yes, but not falling."

Eric ran to the window. "No, I was sure I saw it. Look— there it is!"

Jimmy and Mrs. Holloway went to the window with him. There, in the distant sky, was a small oval object with tail fins.

"That's a blimp!" Jimmy said.

"An easy mistake," Mrs. Holloway said. "You two did very well in the duck and cover drill. Very well indeed. Now let's get that projector and get back to class."

His classmates were jabbering away when Jimmy got back to class, and Mrs. Holloway let them talk while she set up the film.

Ralph leaned forward. "Hey, you're not dead!"

"No, and neither is anybody else."

"What are you talking about?"

"We didn't know it was a drill! We were still ducking and covering when Mrs. Holloway came and got us!"

Ralph had himself a good laugh over that, and Jimmy punched him in the arm.

"It's not funny!"

"Hey, okay, okay. So does that mean Eric is still after you?"

Jimmy looked across the room to where Eric was laughing with his friends, probably telling them all about how he beat up little Jimmy Flint. Somehow he doubted he was telling them how the two of them ducked and covered the rest of the time, thinking it was the end of everything.

"No," Jimmy said. "I think it's over."

✤ ✤ ✤

But it wasn't. On the way home from school that afternoon Eric and his buddies caught Jimmy and Ralph on the cement playground and surrounded them.

"Heya, Skinflint," Eric said. "It's time to finish what we started."

Jimmy couldn't believe it. Not after what they'd been

through, not after what they thought had happened. It's not like he and Eric had become buddies hiding under the table, but Jimmy figured it had shown both of them there were bigger things to worry about than who beat who at card flipping.

Eric cracked his knuckles. "Now, where were we?"

Jimmy backed up, but one of Eric's buddies shoved him forward. If Jimmy didn't think of something fast, he was going to get it. He looked around frantically for a teacher, a parent, but there was nobody around. There *was* something in the sky, though—

"Look! Up in the sky! It's a bomb!"

"What? Huh? Where?" Eric's gang said, and everyone looked where Jimmy was pointing.

"That's not a bomb, you moron!" one of Eric's buddies said. "That's a blimp!"

"The spaz don't even know the difference between a blimp and a bomb!"

Eric's gang broke up in fits of laughter, but Jimmy saw right away that Eric wasn't laughing. He was glaring at Jimmy, warning him silently with his eyes not to say anything more.

"Did you see a flash? They said there'd be a flash. Are you sure you didn't see it?" he said, overplaying it so he was sure Eric got the message. From the scowl on Eric's face, Jimmy knew he understood. If Eric beat him up, Jimmy would tell everybody how he'd ducked and covered, and mistaken a blimp for a bomb. He might still put Jimmy in a body cast, but Eric's reputation as a tough guy would be ruined forever. It felt wrong to make fun of Eric for being scared. Jimmy had been just as frightened, maybe even more so. But Jimmy wasn't the one picking the fight.

"Come on, Eric, pound him!" one of the boys said.

Eric sneered at Jimmy, then gave in. "Not today."

Eric's buddies couldn't believe it.

"Not today, Skinflint," Eric said, pointing a finger at his nose. "But one day, when you least expect it—" He smacked a fist into his open hand. *"Boom."*

He was just making a show of being tough for his gang, and Jimmy didn't say anything more. He didn't have to. He and Eric both knew what would happen if he made good on his threat. And it wasn't just his word against Eric's—Mrs. Holloway knew all about him ducking and covering from a blimp too.

Eric turned and walked away, and his confused friends followed him.

Jimmy let out a breath he didn't realize he'd been holding.

"What—what just happened!?" Ralph asked. "He was gonna pummel you!"

"He was, but it's over. For real, this time."

"What do you mean it's over? He just said one day when you least expect it, boom!"

"He won't do it," Jimmy said. "Not now and not ever."

He looked up into the sky, trying to see Sputnik. "And I don't think the Russians will either." He was beginning to understand now, and it felt like a great weight was lifting off his shoulders.

"What are you talking about?"

Jimmy smiled and told Ralph all about Mutually Assured Destruction as they looked for a place to flip cards.

Eighth Inning: The Perfectionist

Brooklyn, New York, 1981

1

It was shaping up to be a perfect summer day, but Michael Flint didn't notice it. Not right away, at least. He was too focused on perfecting his curveball to notice anything else. His grandma Kat had taught him how to throw one, but he still hadn't mastered it. He was doing everything he was supposed to: He held the ball deep in his palm, he nestled his first two fingers along one of the seams, he rolled his hand to give the ball downspin. But the ball either ended up breaking far too early and bouncing home, or it flattened out and didn't break at all—the dreaded "hanging curveball" that was so easy to hit. Every now and then he got one just right and it dropped into the catcher's mitt like a Tom Seaver curveball, but he couldn't do it perfectly every time and so he *never* did it. At least not in a game.

The rest of the team began to arrive for their morning game at the Prospect Park baseball fields, and Michael and his catcher Carlos Reyes finished up their workout to join them.

"You've just about got that curveball down," Carlos told him.

"Yeah. But not quite."

"When the baseball strike ends, you should watch Fernando Valenzuela throw. He has the best curveball in the majors."

"Fernando has the best *screwball* in the majors."

Carlos grinned. "Yes, but his curveball is the best too."

In the dugout Michael found his closest friend on the team, Adam Rosenfeld, and tossed his glove on the bench beside him. Adam was a curly-headed eleven-year-old from Richmond, Virginia, who could never sit still. He played just about every position on the team, was a star football player, and could beat Michael handily at any video game.

"Me and Raul saw *Raiders of the Lost Ark* last night," he said.

"Again? How many times is that?"

"Seven. How many times you seen *Empire?*"

Michael shrugged. "Ten or twelve."

Coach Clemmons clapped his hands as he came into the wire-fence dugout. "All right, troops, big game today. Big game."

Michael and Adam rolled their eyes at each other. Every game was a "big game" for Coach Clemmons, even though it was the middle of the season.

"Who's ready to get off the schnide? Hmm?" He clapped again. "I want to see some focus out there today, all right, boys?" He made his way down the bench. "Let's take good swings today, all right? Keep your eye on the ball. We're going up against their best pitcher." Coach Clemmons got to Michael. "But they're going up against *our* best pitcher, right, Michael?"

Michael shrugged, even though he knew it was true. They all knew it was true. If the coach could run him out to pitch every game he would, but the league rules wouldn't allow it.

"We've lost three straight," Coach Clemmons told Michael. "I'm counting on you to be our stopper now, all right? And just remember, not every pitch has to be perfect, Mikey. Most batters will get themselves out, and the guys behind you can do the rest, all right? We may not be able to hit a lick, but we can field like nobody's business. All right?"

Michael nodded and Coach Clemmons went back down to the front of the dugout, clapping to rally his team.

"All right, you're our best pitcher now, all right?" Adam said, riffing on Coach Clemmons. "You don't have to be perfect, all right? Just all right. All right?"

Michael held up his hands and laughed. "All right! All right!"

"All right," Adam said.

The Bob Smith Ford team took the field first, and Michael and Adam chatted while their Fulton Street Pawn and Loan teammates took their swings.

"So you've seen *Empire* all those times," Adam said as they watched George Robinson ground out to short. "Who do you think Yoda meant when he said, 'There is another.' You know, when he was talking about other Jedis besides Luke."

"Han Solo. Has to be."

"No way," Carlos said. "He says he doesn't believe in all that stuff."

"So what? He doesn't have to believe in it. The Force is what it is."

"I think it's Lando," Adam said.

"What? No."

"Well who then?"

"I think it's R2-D2," Carlos said.

Michael and Adam busted out laughing.

"You guys settle down back there and focus, all right?" Coach Clemmons called. "Now come on. Let's hear a little baseball chatter, all right?"

Michael wiped tears from his eyes. "Come on batter. Get a hit," he called, trying not to laugh.

"*Um* batter, *um* batter," Adam said, but he was overcome by another laughing fit and had to stop.

"What? Who says R2-D2 can't have the Force?" Carlos said.

"Dude. He's a *robot*. Robots can't have the Force. Only living things."

"Says who?"

The last batter struck out swinging and the bench shuffled to its feet to take the field. Michael shook his head, still laughing, as he climbed up on the mound. He threw a few warm-up tosses and then the first Bob Smith Ford batter stepped up to the plate.

"Easy out, now, easy out," Adam called from first base.

Michael set up his off-speed pitches with his fastball, fast, slow, fast again, and got the lead-off batter to pop out. The second batter saw a steady diet of fastballs, this time in and out, out and in. He struck out swinging on four pitches. The third batter was Bob Smith Ford's best; he'd hit two doubles off Michael last time they'd played, and Michael didn't want to let him do that again. He worked him inside, inside, inside, not letting him get those big long arms around on anything. He got a piece of one that shot a mile in the air and came down in fair territory around third base, where Ramon hauled it in for the last out of the inning.

Back in the dugout Michael started kidding Carlos about C-3PO maybe having the Force. Adam nodded at something behind him.

"Little brother alert," Adam said.

Michael's little brother, David, stood on the other side of the chain-link fence, a messy ice cream cone in his hand and the other half on his face.

Michael sighed. "What?"

"You want to play Atari later?"

"I'm kind of doing something right now, David. I'll worry about that later, all right? Sheesh. Now get out of here."

David stayed where he was and scarfed his ice cream cone.

"Go on, beat it!" Michael said. David turned to go back to the stands. "Wait, wait," Michael said. "Tell Grandma Kat I'm opening up too much on my follow-through and ask her what I should do."

David took another bite of his ice cream cone.

"So go *on*, you little Ugnaught."

David left again.

"What a dork."

"So, you think you'll play Atari later?" Adam asked.

"Yeah. Probably."

Coach Clemmons called Michael out on deck, and he went to the plate to bat when Ramon grounded out. Michael's helmet was a little too big and his bat was a little too small, but he wasn't a very good hitter anyway. Good enough to bat seventh, but that was only because Tim and Alberto were a lot worse.

Michael managed to work a two and two count and got his aluminum bat on the next pitch, but all he did was float a weak liner to second base for the third out. He tossed his bat and helmet back in the dugout and Adam brought his glove out for him as the teams changed sides. The next half inning he made quick work of the Bob Smith Ford batters, notching two strikeouts and a fly ball to right. He still wasn't locating his pitches where he wanted them, though, and David wasn't back when he came off the field. He tried to find his family in the bleachers, but he couldn't see them.

"Useless," Michael said.

The next half inning he went back to the mound to face the bottom three hitters in the Bob Smith Ford lineup. He got a strikeout, a ground out, and then the ninth batter, probably the lamest on the team, made Ramon have to dive to save a sure double down the line. But Ramon was so good and the runner was so slow he still threw him out at first.

Michael threw his glove against the chain-link fence and kicked the dirt floor when he got back to the bench.

"It doesn't have to be perfect," Coach Clemmons called. "Let's show a little respect for the game down there, all right?"

Michael caught sight of his brother on the path behind the dugout and called him over.

"David! David, what did Grandma Kat say?"

David had a little red and white bag of popcorn, and he stuffed a handful in his mouth.

"Abow wha?"

"About me opening up too soon! Not locating my pitches."

"She seb if yow're piding pewfec yow're nob dobing anbyfing wong."

"In *English*, please?"

David swallowed. "She said if you're pitching perfect you're not doing anything wrong."

"But I'm *not* pitching perfect."

"Yes you are," Adam said. "Nobody's reached first base in three innings. That's perfect." Adam laughed. "Hey, just six more innings and you've got a perfect game!"

"Right," Michael said. Like he could *ever* be perfect.

2

Fulton Street Pawn and Loan didn't score in their bottom half of the inning, even though they did muster two hits. In the bottom of the fourth Michael faced the other team's top three hitters again, registering a strikeout and a ground out to Adam for the first two outs of the inning. Then the big doubles hitter came to the plate, and Michael knew he wouldn't fall for a barrage of inside pitches again. He looked in to see what Carlos was thinking.

Carlos put down the sign for an inside fastball.

Michael sighed. With just a fastball and a changeup, his off-speed pitch, he didn't have many options. He nodded to Carlos. Even if they didn't go there the entire at bat, he could throw an inside fastball that at least set the batter up, make him think that's what they were going to do again this time.

But Michael didn't want to "waste" a pitch—to throw one that did nothing but delay confrontation. Instead he aimed for the edge of the plate, looking maybe to get a called strike if the umpire was in a generous mood and the big hitter was expecting junk.

The hitter took the pitch. "Strike one!" the umpire cried. The big guy slumped his shoulders and looked back at the umpire, questioning the call without saying a word. His coach said something about it, though, giving the umpire an earful from the dugout.

Carlos threw the ball back to Michael and he looked in again. Fastball inside. Michael shook his head. Carlos wanted a repeat of the first at bat, but Michael knew this guy wouldn't let another close strike go by without doing something with it, and he wasn't going to swing at something too far in. Behind the plate, Carlos shrugged, as if to say, "Okay, what then?"

Carlos put down the sign for a fastball away. Michael nodded. It was worth a shot, and the hitter might be expecting more inside stuff. But Michael would really have to waste one now. If he put it anywhere near the plate the hitter would tattoo it to right field.

Michael took a deep breath, aimed, and let his fastball fly. The hitter was ready for it, eager for anything he could reach out for, and he lunged after the fastball like a golfer.

"Strike two!" the umpire called. Michael snapped the ball back in his glove and nodded to Carlos. They had the guy on the ropes. He peered in for the sign.

Carlos dropped two fingers.

The curveball? Was Carlos crazy? A third of the time it

bounced to the plate, and a third of the time it floated in like the fattest, most hittable pitch the batter had ever seen. Sure, there was that other third of the time when it broke just right, when it came in looking like a fastball and then dove away at the last second, leaving batters flailing, but there was no way he could take the chance. He shook Carlos off.

Carlos's catcher's mask tilted sideways, and Michael knew he was wondering: "If not now, when?"

Michael sighed again. Carlos was right, and he knew it. The pitch wouldn't *get* to be perfect if he didn't use it, and a two-strike count was the time to try it. He motioned for Carlos to cycle through the pitches one more time and nodded at the sign for curveball.

"Drop in there," Michael whispered as he went into his windup. "Drop in there drop in there drop in there."

He released, staring the ball down as it flew closer, closer, closer—

—but didn't drop. It hung like a fat breaking ball, and the big Bob Smith Ford hitter took a late, greedy hack at it. The ball pinged off his bat and flew straight back into the chain-link fence backstop behind the plate—*thwack!*—rattling the No Pepper sign.

The big hitter glanced back at Michael like he couldn't believe the gift he'd just been given, and he kicked at the dirt for not blasting the ball for a home run.

"All right, enough of that, then," Michael said. He got a new ball from Carlos and they went back to square one.

Another fastball away? No. Another fastball inside? No. An off-speed pitch *way* outside? *No.* Everybody always wanted to waste pitches when they had a two-strike count, like they had three balls they could throw anywhere. What was the point of wasting a good count just to run it back to three balls and two strikes?

Carlos called time-out and jogged to the mound.

"You gotta call something, amigo. I say try the curveball again."

"No," Michael said. He grasped for something, anything he could use to get him out. "Changeup low. Bottom of the strike zone."

"Why not waste a couple first? Get him guessing."

Michael shook his head. "He's too smart for that. Let's go with the low changeup."

Carlos shrugged and jogged back to the plate, and Michael kneaded the ball in his hands. When his catcher was set he went into his windup, then slowed his delivery down, aiming for the bottom of the strike zone. The ball took an eternity to get there, and he watched as he followed through. The hitter waited, waited, waited, hitched his shoulder, then swung—

The bat met the ball with the resounding *ping* of aluminum, but he drove the ball down, into the ground. It tore a divot in the earth four feet in front of home and bounced to short, where George made quick work of it and threw the batter out at first. Michael pumped his fist and slapped Carlos on the back as they ran back in the dugout, four innings in the books.

Four perfect innings.

Michael was up first for Fulton Street Pawn and Loan, and he grabbed his helmet and bat and walked out to the plate while the other pitcher took a few warm-up tosses. Perfect through four innings. That was something, but a lot of pitchers had been perfect for four innings. Perfect for nine innings was a different thing altogether. There had only been ten perfect games in the history of Major League Baseball. Grandma Kat loved to tell the story of being there for Sandy Koufax's perfect game in 1965, but good as he was, Sandy Koufax had never thrown another. Tom Seaver and a host of others hadn't thrown *any*.

A perfect game was practically impossible, wasn't it? Especially for Michael. He'd walk someone, or there would be a bloop hit, or one of his teammates would throw one three feet over Adam's head at first for an error. Besides, none of that was going to matter if they didn't get some runs. The score was still 0–0.

Michael did his best at the plate, but the pitcher was too good for him. Even when he could guess what was coming he still couldn't do much with it, grounding back out to the mound and getting tossed out easily at first.

Coach Clemmons clapped as he ran back into the dugout—Coach Clemmons clapped for everything, from a home run to a strikeout—but nobody said anything to Michael as he made his way down to the end of the bench. He sat next to Adam and Carlos, but neither of them said anything either.

"So I've got another idea," Michael said. "About who the other Jedi is." He paused, trying to build suspense for his punchline. "It's Chewbacca!"

Michael grinned, expecting Adam to laugh and Carlos to get upset that they were still making fun of him, but Adam just looked at his feet and Carlos worked at cleaning the dirt from his cleats.

"It could be Chewbacca," Adam said.

Michael looked around at his friends. What was wrong with them? Had he done something to make them mad?

Before he could ask, the last batter of the inning struck out and Coach Clemmons was rallying everyone back out onto the field. Michael walked up on the mound, still wondering what he'd said to make his friends upset. But if something was wrong Carlos didn't show it behind the plate. He was all business as the bottom half of the inning got going, and they made quick work of the next three batters in the lineup, setting them down one-two-three.

Coach Clemmons clapped as Michael ran past him into the dugout, but he didn't say anything. The whole bench was quiet, and Adam and Carlos sat near Michael but wouldn't even look at him. Michael's little brother, David, standing right beyond the chain-link fence and eating a Moon Pie, was the only one who even acknowledged his presence.

"Everybody's talking about you," David said.

"What?"

"In the stands. Everybody is talking about your perfect game."

Adam and Carlos glared at David, but said nothing. So *that's* what this was about. His teammates all knew he had a perfect game through five innings, and nobody wanted to say or do anything to jinx it.

"Mr. Robinson says it's impossible."

"Shut up," Michael said.

"Dad thinks you can do it, though."

"Shut up," he said, Adam and Carlos joining him this time. His friends frowned at Michael as if to say, "Don't jinx it!"

Coach Clemmons called Carlos's name, and he got up to go hit.

"I'm telling Mom you told me to shut up."

"So go tell her and leave me alone!"

David turned to go.

"Wait!"

Michael ignored the glare from Adam and went to the back corner of the dugout to whisper through the fence with David. "What does Grandma Kat say?"

David shrugged.

"Ask her what she thinks I should do about that big guy, their number three hitter. I have to get him out one more time. Ask her what I should do."

David took another bite of his Moon Pie.

"So go already!"

David wandered off, and Michael watched as Carlos hit into a double play. Four pitches later Ramon was down on strikes and the half inning was over. It was time for Michael to face the bottom of the sixth.

He walked out to his position more slowly this time, trying to calm down and think about how he was going to get the next three batters out. It was the bottom three hitters again, but Michael didn't want to fall asleep and let one of them sneak something by like the ninth batter almost had last time. Michael climbed the mound and took off his hat to wipe the sweat away. It was mid-morning now, and the summer sun was shining right down on him. He looked around at the bleachers to find his family and realized for the first time that the crowd was larger than it had been before. The stands were full, and there were people scattered up and down the foul lines.

And they were all looking for perfection.

Michael pulled his cap back down tight and looked in at Carlos. The first batter they worked up and in, up and in, and then down and away. Strikeout. The next batter swung at the first pitch and drove it to right. The crowd gasped and Michael's heart skipped a beat, but then he saw it was routine and watched as Raul put it away. After his near heart attack, Michael vowed to put the last batter away without letting him make contact, and he struck him out on five pitches.

The crowd burst into applause at the strikeout, surprising Michael and his teammates. There were even more people watching now, people who must have come from one of the other six Prospect Park fields where games were being played. Michael and his teammates stood at their positions for a few seconds, unsure of how to handle their newfound attention, then came to their senses and ran off the field.

Michael now had no company at the end of the bench, silent or otherwise. Adam and Carlos found excuses to be at the far end of the dugout, and Michael sat all alone. It wouldn't have mattered anyway. The dugout was as quiet as a classroom during a test.

"All right, boys," Coach Clemmons said, breaking the strange silence. "Top of the seventh. I don't think I need to tell anyone how much we need a run right now, do I?"

Nobody answered.

"All right then. Let's do it. And come on, I want to hear a little chatter in here. I want everybody to loosen up, all right? Who's seen that new *Clash of the Titans* movie, huh?"

Michael had seen it, but he didn't want to talk about it. Neither did anybody else on the team, it seemed. All he could think about was the perfect game. Where was David? Had he gone to talk to Grandma Kat, or was he off at the concession stand again? Michael took off his hat and rubbed at his temples. He wanted this, wanted perfection more than anything. A perfect game, and he was three innings away. But how would he get through that lineup one more time?

The Fulton Street Pawn and Loan lead-off hitter drew a walk, then stole second. It was the first runner they'd had in scoring position all game, but Michael was only half paying attention. In his mind, he was going over every pitch he had thrown that game to every batter. How had he gotten the number two batter out in the fourth? What had the number six hitter done with the off-speed pitch he'd thrown him in the second? Michael closed his eyes and tried to think. *Think.* What could he do to keep things perfect? He did *not* want to screw this up.

A bunt got the runner to third as Michael hurried down the bench to Tim's little brother, Chris, who kept score for the team.

"I need to see the scorebook," Michael told him.

Chris was a few years younger than Michael, maybe nine like David, and he was usually quiet around the older kids on the team. Now a thirteen-year-old was talking to him, and Michael wasn't just any thirteen-year-old: He was the one pitching a perfect game, the one nobody wanted to talk to.

Chris looked to the other boys for help, but nobody would look at him.

"I—I—" he started, then just handed Michael the book, despite the fact that he should be recording the run Fulton Street Pawn and Loan was scoring right then off a sacrifice fly.

The crowd cheered the run but Michael ignored them, poring over the ledger for the other team. Strikeout, ground-out, pop foul, strikeout—the scorebook wouldn't tell him the pitches he'd thrown, just the outcomes, but he could reconstruct the rest himself. As he stared at the boxes on the page, the impossibility of it all stood out even more. Out, out, out, out . . . eighteen boxes, eighteen hitters, eighteen outs. Not one person had reached first base. No hits, no errors, no walks. No hitter had even gotten to a full count. The enormity of it, the craziness of it, was almost overwhelming.

The half inning ended without another run scoring, but Fulton Street Pawn and Loan now led one to nothing. Coach Clemmons came back into the dugout clapping.

"All right," he told his team. "All right!" He looked at Michael. *"All right."*

Any other day the boys would have been laughing, but not today. Michael understood what his coach meant. The team had gotten Michael his one run, the one run he needed to win, and that was all he was going to get.

Now it was up to him to go out and be perfect.

3

Carlos put down two fingers, asking for the curveball. Michael wanted to call time-out and kill him.

Instead he shook him off—vigorously this time, hoping he got the point. Carlos slouched again and went through the other signals, trying to find something they could both agree on. Michael already had two outs in the seventh inning. The last batter he had to retire was the big number three hitter, and they were running out of things to throw him. Michael took a deep breath, wishing he'd heard back from Grandma Kat before the start of the half inning.

Carlos put down a single finger—a fastball—but didn't indicate left or right. A fastball, right down the middle, to Bob Smith Ford's best hitter. Well, it was something he certainly wouldn't expect, but he was too good a hitter not to do something with it, even if he didn't see it coming. No, Michael would nibble at the corners of the strike zone before he gave him a fat fastball to hit.

He took a sign he liked from Carlos and pitched. He

meant it to be low and inside, but it wasn't perfect. The ball came back toward the plate more than he meant it to, and he watched in horror as the big hitter attacked it, driving the ball deep to right center. Raul broke right and Tim Clemmons in center broke left, and the big crowd sitting in the bleachers rose to their feet. All Michael could do was watch as the ball sailed farther and farther and Raul and Tim drew closer and closer—then Raul was sliding out of the way so he wouldn't hit Tim, and Tim was reaching as high and far as he could, and both players went tumbling as the ball disappeared between them.

And then Tim Clemmons popped up triumphantly with the ball clutched in his glove. The umpire, who'd run all the way out past second base to watch, signaled "out" with his fist. The audience cheered, and Michael waited on the infield to rub Tim's hat around on his head in thanks.

Twenty-one outs. Six more to go.

Michael went to his solitary place at the end of the bench and the wall of silence descended again between him and his teammates. They sat so far away now Michael felt like he had some disease no one else wanted to get. No one but David, who stood behind him eating a snow cone.

"There's a reporter here," David said. "From the *Canarsie Courier.* Somebody called him."

"David, what did Grandma Kat say? You talked to her, right?"

David shrugged. "She said you had to just keep doing whatever it was you were doing."

Michael grabbed the chain-link fence in his fingers and rattled it. "That's not good enough!" he said, drawing stares from a couple of his teammates, who just as quickly looked away. Michael lowered his voice. "David, I can't just keep doing what I've been doing. They've seen it all before, and my arm is getting tired. What am I supposed to do?"

"I dunno," David said. He shrugged again and took a bite of his snow cone.

If the chain-link fence hadn't been there Michael would *so* have killed his brother. Instead he tried to calm himself down. He could kill David *after* the game.

"Just . . . Look, tell her to come down here, all right? Tell her I need to talk to her."

David took another bite of his snow cone and walked away.

"Adopted. He has to be adopted," Michael muttered.

His turn to bat came up again that inning, but this time he didn't care. He took his bat and his helmet and stood in the batter's box, but he was hardly aware of the pitches coming his way. Instead he was looking at the players in the field he knew he had to face again. The third baseman, the shortstop, the pitcher, the left fielder, the right fielder, the second baseman. What did he know about each of them that he could use to get them out? And were they looking at him right now, trying to figure out how they were going to get a hit?

The umpire called strike three and Michael walked back to the dugout, where Coach Clemmons was clapping and exhorting the next batter to get a hit, ignoring Michael completely. He didn't care. He didn't want to talk to anybody anyway.

One out later Michael was back on the mound. Foul territory was now full of people, the crowd so large there was an audible murmur from them. The opposing coach clapped and urged his players to get a hit. Michael's own teammates stood silently behind him, waiting for whatever would come.

Michael squeezed the ball in his hand so tightly it hurt. He worried that he didn't have enough gas left, that he didn't have any more tricks up his sleeve, that he'd make a mistake or somebody would get lucky. That he would be a failure in the eyes of however many hundreds of people were watching. He called time-out and walked around the mound once more, but Carlos didn't run out to meet with him and none of the infielders came in to talk to him. He was in this alone.

The ump gave him a moment, then Michael stepped back up and went at it. He got a fly ball to second from the first batter, a strikeout of the second, and a ground ball to third for the last hitter, and suddenly the inning was over, as easy as any he'd ever pitched.

And he was three outs from perfection.

The crowd cheered as he walked off the field, but he could

sense the expectation in their voices. He went back and sat by himself at the end of the bench, wondering again if he had what it took to be perfect.

David appeared again, eating a hot dog.

"David! Where's Grandma Kat?"

"She won't come."

"What!?"

"She says you're not supposed to talk to somebody with a perfect game. She won't even say 'perfect game.' She just keeps working her way up and down the bleachers, touching all the wood."

Michael leaned close to the fence to whisper to his brother. "I'm running out of ideas here, David. I don't know how I'm going to get the next three batters out. I don't even know how I got the *last* three batters out. She didn't say *anything?*"

David took a bite of his hot dog and chewed on it, and Michael wished he could choke people with the Force like Darth Vader.

David finally swallowed. "She said there's a time and place for everything."

"That's it? 'There's a time and place for everything'? What's that supposed to mean?"

David shrugged. "So you think you'll play Atari later?"

Michael didn't even bother to answer. On the field behind him, Adam grounded into the last out of the inning, and it was time for Michael to take the mound one last time. He looked around at the empty bench. The team had already left without him, none of them wanting to be the one to jinx it by jostling him or talking to him. Coach Clemmons opened his mouth to say something to him as he passed, but instead just nodded. Michael walked out to the mound.

The crowd burst into applause as he came out of the dugout, and he wondered if he was supposed to tip his cap. That didn't feel right, though, like he'd be thanking them for applause he hadn't earned yet. Instead he went to the mound and took a few light tosses with Carlos. The umpire seemed ready to give Michael as much time as he needed, but Michael just wanted to get it over with. He signaled the umpire he was ready, and the ump called, "Play ball!"

Michael Flint felt like the loneliest boy in all of Brooklyn. He scratched at the dirt of the mound with his cleat, raised his glove to just under his eyes, and stared in at his catcher's signal. He turned, stepped, and threw, threw as hard as he possibly could, and the ball flashed, a brilliant white thing in the midday sun, rocketing toward the catcher's mitt . . . and then over the catcher's mitt, and over the umpire, and into the backstop behind, where it *thwacked* into a pole.

The crowd murmured, and Michael could hear their words in his head. *He's cracking. He's lost it. He can't be perfect.*

Carlos threw him a new ball and Michael worked it over in his hands while trying to clear away the voices in his head. Those weren't the voices of the crowd. He couldn't really hear them. They were the voices inside him, telling him he couldn't do it. But why couldn't he? He didn't know what he was doing that was different from any other time he'd pitched, but even so the magic had been there all day long. Why did it have to stop? He stepped off the mound, taking the time the umpire had been willing to give him before, and readjusted his hat while he gathered his thoughts. Maybe today was one of those days where everything just clicked. Maybe it had nothing to do with him at all.

Maybe today was perfect.

Michael climbed back up on the mound and shook off Carlos's signals until he had the one he wanted. After the first blazing pitch into the backstop, the hitter was expecting more of the same, so Michael threw the next pitch as slow as he could, aiming it right for the middle of the plate. The batter whiffed on it early enough to swing twice if he wanted to, and the crowd *oohed*. One ball and one strike. Now that the batter was off balance, Michael gave him another changeup—strike two—and then the high heat to finish him off.

Two outs to go.

The next batter was a pinch hitter, somebody he hadn't seen before, but the kind of guy who's not a starter for a reason. He flailed at the first pitch, and Carlos wisely called for a pitch away and Michael got him fishing again for strike two. Ahead 0 and 2, Michael threw the kid an inside pitch that was impossible to hit but he swung at it anyway, strike three.

One out to go. One batter left.

Michael turned around on the mound, facing the outfield and his teammates. They watched him now, stared at him, and he could feel the eyes of everyone in Prospect Park. It was like they were holding their collective breath, waiting to see if perfection was possible. Michael couldn't decide if he wanted to know the answer or not, but he couldn't just walk away. He had to finish the game, one way or another. He turned and faced home plate and a new pinch hitter.

His first pitch was a fastball, and the batter took it for strike one. Michael felt a surge of optimism. Maybe it was possible. Maybe he could be perfect. He just needed to push it that last little bit.

He got the ball back and sent another fastball toward the plate, this one too high and too fast, so high and fast Carlos had to go up to get it. Michael lost his hat throwing it, and the batter didn't bite. Michael was pressing now and he knew it, grabbing at the magic rather than letting it work on its own, but he was desperate.

Michael got the ball back and picked up his hat, dusting it off. He pulled it back down over his mop of sweaty hair and took another deep breath, his grandmother's lone piece of advice coming back to him.

There's a time and place for everything.

Michael reached back, grabbed for some of that magic, but threw another fastball high. Ball two. He was going to be patient, this batter, make Michael work for it. The Bob Smith Ford coach had saved his best for last.

Michael could feel the sweat running down his back. He had put everything he had into those last two pitches, and he didn't have anything more. His fastballs were starting to feel like changeups, huge red and white targets that were as slow as Christmas coming. He couldn't speed it up, and he couldn't slow it down any further. This was it. This was all he had left.

Two balls and one strike. Michael couldn't afford another ball called here, so he took a little something off—though not so much as to make it a proper changeup—and aimed for the corner of the plate. A swing and a miss! He'd evened the count to two balls and two strikes.

If ever there was a time to waste a pitch, this was it, but Michael still refused. If he threw a wide pitch well outside the strike zone, there was little chance this hitter would chase it, and all that would do would force the issue next pitch on a full count, where the batter knew he couldn't make a mistake, wouldn't throw a ball. Michael waved off the waste-pitch signal Carlos gave him and nodded for the inside fastball. He'd try to hit the corner, catch him looking.

His arms like rubber, his legs like logs, Michael stepped into his windup and pitched it right where he wanted it, the magic back. The batter flinched but didn't swing. The ball popped into Carlos's mitt. Michael felt relief beyond relief, could see now what kind of day it was, a *perfect* day, and started to jump for joy—

And the umpire called the pitch a ball.

The crowd booed and hissed, but Michael knew it had been a close one. He'd put it out on the edge hoping for a strike, the kind of pitch that had to be perfect.

But he wasn't perfect. He was never going to *be* perfect. He had twenty-six outs, three balls, and two strikes, and he was as close to perfection—and imperfection—as he was ever going to get. If he could freeze that moment, preserve it, he could forever be one strike away from glory, the applause for what he was *doing* never-ending, the disappointment for what he had *not* done never felt.

And that was when Michael Flint noticed what kind of day it was.

He had glimpsed it a few seconds before when he'd thought the game was over, when he'd truly relaxed for the first time all day. He looked for it again now and there it was, all around him. The kind of day where a little dirt on his hands felt good, where the high blue sky was just right for catching fly balls, where grounders always bounced into his outstretched glove. It had been that way all along, but it hadn't belonged to him or to anybody else. It was *baseball's* day, a day when the Earth said, "Here's the best I've got," and baseball said, *"That's pretty good, Earth, but I'll show you* perfect."

It was a day like Michael had never known and knew he would never see again. Like Sandy Koufax and his perfect game, it was a special gift in a special time and a special place, one that he shouldn't examine too closely, one he could never duplicate. No matter how much he worked, no matter hard he tried, it was the kind of perfect day that would come only when *it* wanted to, when the sun smiled and the grass laughed and wind sang *hm-batter-hm-batter-hm-batter-swing*.

It wasn't up to Michael anymore. He saw that now. He stepped back up on the mound, worked his fingers into the right grip, shook Carlos off until he dropped two fingers for a curve, and let the ball fly.

Ninth Inning: Provenance

Brooklyn, New York, 2002

1

The room was on fire.

That's the way it looked through Snider Flint's blurry eyes. He woke in a sweat to a piercing alarm, louder and harsher than his bedside alarm clock. *The smoke detector.* He snapped awake, feeling the full blast of heat on his face, seeing the orange flames licking up under his bedroom door, through his walls. *Through his walls?* Was that even possible?

He scrambled back on his bed, away from his door. Smoke collected on the ceiling in great billowing clouds, as though it were some kind of monster, alive. Snider coughed and slid off the end of his bed to get away from the black air.

"Mom?" he called, choking. "Dad!?"

The window *thump-thump-thumped* behind him and he jumped.

"Snider! Snider, wake up!" It was his father, standing on the porch roof just beneath Snider's second-story window. He had his hand to the glass, trying to see in. "Snider, the house is on fire! You've got to crawl out the window!"

Snider stood where his father could see him, covering his mouth and nose with the sleeve of his T-shirt while he wrangled the difficult latch on the top of his casement window. It finally gave, and he hefted the heavy old window up enough to crawl through. In the distance, Snider could hear the siren of a fire engine and realized it was coming for *his* house.

"What happened?" Snider asked as his father helped him onto the roof. "Where's Mom?"

"She's already out. The Hendersons are helping her get down. Are you all right?"

Snider coughed again and nodded. Heat radiated from the house behind them, making his eyes burn. Glass tinkled and shattered.

"Come on, let's get out of here," his father said. Snider held his father's hand as they inched their way barefoot down the rough shingles, the fire hissing and roaring behind them.

Snider's dad slipped. He hit the roof with a *thump*, letting go of Snider to throw his arms out and catch himself. Snider tried to grab him and lost his footing too. His father flattened himself out on the roof and slid to a stop, but Snider skidded on past, out of reach. He rolled over on his stomach and clawed, kicked, dragged, but he kept sliding sickeningly down, down, down.

There were screams below—his mother, the neighbors—but they were as helpless as Snider as his feet caught on the gutter and then hammered past, his weight and speed too much for it to stop him. Half off the roof, half on, Snider grabbed for the gutter, but the flimsy metal thing ripped away from the wall and Snider went spinning, falling, into darkness.

Snider cried out and woke in a sweat to the memory of falling and fire. He shot straight up, his sheets already a tangled mess at his feet, casting around in the dark to figure out where he was.

"Snider. Snider, it's all right. You're all right," a voice said. It was Snider's uncle Dave, and Snider immediately remembered where he was. This was Dave's little apartment above his antiques store. An electrical fire in the old wiring in Snider's house had burned it to the ground, and Uncle Dave was sharing his place with Snider and his parents while they continued the impossible search for an affordable apartment to rent while their new house was being built. Snider was on the living room couch and Dave was beside him on the floor on an air mattress. Snider's parents slept in Dave's bedroom.

"Do you need anything?" Uncle Dave asked. "A glass of water?"

"No," Snider said. He turned over and buried his face in the back of the couch, ashamed that his uncle had heard him screaming again. He hated that he didn't have a room of his own anymore, that everything he owned was stuffed into a duffel bag at the end of the couch, that it was impossible to be alone. It wasn't his uncle's fault, but he still wished he was anywhere else but here.

Snider pulled the blanket back up over the cast on his broken leg and tried to sleep, praying he didn't dream of fire again.

✢ ✢ ✢

Dave's two-room apartment was never smaller than when he and Snider's parents were all getting ready to leave for work in the morning. Snider kept his blanket pulled up over his head as they came in and out of the bathroom, bustled about the kitchen, and watched the morning news where he pretended to sleep.

"Snider," his mother said, "I want you to be ready to go to Paramus this afternoon."

"I don't want to go to New Jersey," he mumbled.

"You need a whole new set of clothes."

"Where am I going to put them? On top of the TV? Under the couch?"

"We're all having to make sacrifices, Snider. Your uncle David most of all. You're just going to have to get used to not living on your own terms, at least for another year."

Snider sat up. "Another year? But the insurance people said they could have a new place built in six months."

"That's if we want one of those contemporary in-fill monstrosities. We're having them rebuild the old house instead."

"Rebuild the old house? You've got to be crazy!" Snider

maneuvered his broken leg on the couch while his mother went around the room assembling the things she needed to take to work. "It was too small. And too old. It's like we were living in an ancient ruin. I just thought we couldn't afford to move."

"Your uncle David and I grew up in that house, Snider. It meant a lot to me," his dad said.

Dave stood in the kitchen and sipped from a mug of coffee, listening to the argument.

"So wait," Snider said. "People are paying all kinds of money to tear down old houses like ours and build *new* ones, and you're going to have them build the same old house when you could have something bigger and modern for *free?*"

"In-fill housing ruins neighborhoods, Snider. And besides, it's ugly."

"This is so lame! And you don't care that this is going to take an entire year? I'll have to start high school somewhere else. I'll miss my freshman year with my friends!"

His mother sighed. "We're in *Fort Greene,* Snider, not Hoboken. You'll see your friends plenty. And we're *trying* to find a place to rent in Flatbush. Now will you please be ready to go to Paramus this afternoon?"

"I'm getting all Mets jerseys."

"You're getting *no* Mets jerseys," his mother said.

"Three Mets jerseys."

"One Mets jersey."

"Two Mets jerseys."

"Two Mets jerseys, and not a single complaint when we try on dress clothes."

"Whatever," Snider said.

His parents left for work, and Snider hopped over to Dave's computer to check on his fantasy baseball team and to see if any of his friends were awake and online. Nobody was up, of course. Why would they be? It was summer, and none of them had to sleep in the same room where their parents made toast. Most of them wouldn't be online later either. They'd be out at the pool or at the ball field or the park. Snider *thunked* his way back over to the couch and started flipping through the cable channels, ready for another exciting day of watching ESPN News for Mets highlights.

Uncle Dave finished cleaning up from breakfast and came into the living room, where he picked up the TV remote and turned it off.

"Hey, what gives?"

"Come down and see me in the shop when you're showered and dressed," Dave said, leaving before Snider could argue.

✤ ✤ ✤

Snider *ka-thunked* his way down the narrow back staircase to Dave's shop. The small storage area at the bottom was a cluttered mess, like a single attic with the junk of an entire neighborhood piled up to the ceiling. Among the stacks Snider saw an old bugle, a Japanese sword on a stand, and an ancient-looking game console with dials instead of joysticks, but rather than stop and look he turned sideways and crab-walked himself on his crutches through the piles of collectibles into the front of the shop, where his uncle Dave sat at a computer entering items for sale into an online auction site. Snider flopped on a stool behind the counter and waited.

Uncle Dave spared him a glance over his shoulder, then kept working.

"Pretty rough on your parents back there, weren't you?"

Snider huffed. "Is that what this is? The part where you tell me how much my parents love me and how tough this is for them too?"

Dave swiveled in his chair. "No. This is the part where I tell you to get over it."

"What?"

"It's time for you to get over the fire, to get over your broken leg and your lost summer, and start pulling your weight around here."

Snider burned with shame and anger that his uncle would bring up the fire.

"Look—"

"No, *you* look. Your parents are both working full-time jobs while they haggle with insurance agents, comb Flatbush for an apartment big enough to live in and cheap enough to actually pay for, meet with architects and builders, and reconstruct your lives. What have you been doing?"

"I'm fourteen. What *can* I do?"

"What are you good at?"

"Baseball."

"Too bad. Your leg's broken. What else?"

Snider shifted uncomfortably. "Video games," he said, just to be perverse.

"Great. Maybe we can put you to work crafting shirts in an online game and sell the gold you make to other players."

"Ha-ha."

"Or wait," Dave said. "I've got a better idea." He stood and handed Snider a broom. "Clean out the back room."

"Hello? Broken leg, remember?" he said, rattling his crutches.

"All right. Fine. Here," Dave said, plunking a cardboard box in front of Snider. "You like working on the computer so much, use it to find out how much this stuff is worth."

"Whatever," Snider said.

Uncle Dave gave his seat at the computer to Snider and went to work in the back room. Snider rolled his eyes at the box and opened it. It was a lot of baseball junk at least, but most of it wasn't anything to get excited about: a moldy old catcher's mitt, a used scorebook, a silly-looking beauty guide for an all-girls baseball league.

There was also an old wooden bat, and a baseball that should have been thrown in the trash a long time ago. The baseball was made of dark brown leather, almost black, with white stitches instead of red. The seams didn't go in a wavy pattern either, they were sewn in an X shape. The stitches were all torn up, though, and two of the leather flaps were so loose Snider could see the wound string inside the ball. One of the flaps had a little letter *S* scratched into it too.

Snider surfed the Net for a half an hour, found some comparable junk, typed up prices for the stuff in the box, and printed it out.

"Here," he said. He handed the sheet to his uncle and went back upstairs to see if the afternoon Mets game was on yet.

2

The next morning Snider settled onto the stool behind the counter of Fulton Street Antiques and Collectibles wearing his new Mike Piazza Mets jersey. Uncle Dave was talking to an actual customer—something even more rare than the baseball cards in his display case—about an old lunch box.

"A Jetsons lunch box," the customer said. "What a fabulous piece!"

"It's a 1963 original," Dave told him. "Hardly any scratches on it. Just a little normal wear around the edges. The sticker is the original Aladdin sticker. No rust on the thermos inside, cup and stopper in pristine condition."

The customer turned the lunch box over in his hands. "What are you asking?"

"Eight hundred."

Snider nearly fell off his stool, but the customer nodded like that was about what he expected. He handed the lunch box back to Uncle Dave.

"It's great stuff," the man said. "I don't suppose you have a Star Trek lunch box, do you? One of the 1968 ones, with the *Enterprise* on one side and the picture of Kirk and Spock beaming out on the side?"

"No, I'm sorry."

The customer smiled. "I had one of those when I was in fourth grade. I loved that thing. I remember, Friday nights I was allowed to stay up late and watch TV. I'd watch *The Wild, Wild West,* then flip the station to *Star Trek.*"

"Good stuff," Dave said.

"I have no idea what happened to that lunch box. I'm sure my mom just threw it out. Anyway, thanks a lot."

"You bet," Uncle Dave said. He put the Jetsons lunchbox back on a shelf as the customer left.

"Not the right price?" Snider asked.

"Not the right lunch box," Dave said. "Most collectors, they collect things because they have a sentimental value to them. The comic book collector whose parents never let him read comics when he was a kid, that guy who remembers watching *Star Trek.*" Dave smiled. "The antiques store owner who never got over selling all his Star Wars toys at a garage sale when he was fourteen. Didn't you lose anything in the fire you can't replace?"

"No."

"I see. So, to what do I owe the pleasure of your visit this morning?" Dave asked.

"The TV remote has mysteriously disappeared."

"Why not just get up and change the channel whenever you want? Oh—right. Your broken leg. Bummer. Well, since you're here—"

Dave slapped the price sheet Snider had typed up onto the counter in front of him.

"What? You said look up what the stuff was worth, so I did."

"Come on—this is price guide stuff. A third grader could have done this. Here, look at this baseball," he said, pulling it out of the box. "I don't just want to know how old this is. Who used it? How was it made? Who owned it before us, and before that, and before that? Or this bat. Whose was it? Was it used in a game? What's this on the handle—postage stamps? Why are there postage stamps on a bat handle? Where's your natural curiosity?"

"Well, I *am* curious about what happened to the TV remote."

Uncle Dave ignored that. "Who wore this cap? Did the Knickerbockers use this ball?"

"The who?"

"The first modern baseball team." Uncle Dave pulled each piece out of the box and laid them on the counter. "You find the provenance of something, its origin, you start to find its story. You find its story, you find its *real* value. Here." Uncle Dave took a pair of cleats off a hook on the wall. "Just a crusty old pair of cleats, right? If these had belonged to your dad when he was a kid, they would have been thrown out a long time ago and they'd be rotting in some landfill. Who wants to own Michael Flint's old shoes, right?"

Snider shrugged.

"Okay, so ordinarily, these shoes are worthless. But what if I told you they were worn by Pelé in his very last professional game with the New York Cosmos?"

"Who?"

"Pelé? The greatest soccer star in history?"

Snider shrugged. Uncle Dave sighed and slid the paper over to Snider. "Okay. How about this: You find the *real* value of anything in that box and I'll give you a ten percent commission on the sale."

Snider perked up. Ten percent of an eight-hundred-dollar lunch box was eighty bucks.

"Twenty percent," he countered.

"Fifteen."

"Done," Snider said.

Uncle Dave shook his head like the thrill of the hunt should have been enough to tempt Snider, but Snider didn't care. Fifteen percent of eight hundred dollars was . . . well, he didn't have a calculator handy, but it was more than eighty bucks.

Snider started with the ball that Uncle Dave had been so crazy about, searching the Internet for any references to old X-seam balls marked with an *S*—or *any* kind of ball marked with an *S*. Nothing. The ball was a dead end, so Snider turned his attention to the bat.

It looked similar to a modern bat, but the handle had a smoother rise to the nub and the barrel had a smaller, fatter sweet spot. The wood was dark brown but faded in spots, and the handle had stains on it like pine tar or something. The bat maker's logo was branded into it just below the sweet spot, the name BABE HERMAN was burned into the barrel, and the crown of the bat looked like it had been chewed on by one of the goats at the Prospect Park Zoo. But the strangest thing about the bat was the remnants of postage stamps Uncle Dave had pointed out. They were glued right to the handle, and there was a faint, illegible address printed off to the side, right on the wood of the bat, as though somebody had just dropped it into a mailbox to send it somewhere.

"Babe Herman." Was that Babe Ruth? Snider thought he remembered "Herman" being part of Babe Ruth's real name, but he didn't want to ask Uncle Dave. A Babe Ruth bat could be worth a fortune! He Googled the name, and was disappointed to see it wasn't Babe Ruth. That was George Herman "Babe" Ruth—that's where he'd heard Herman. This was another guy named Babe Herman who played around the same time for the Brooklyn Dodgers, only for some reason they were called the Brooklyn Robins then. Best he could tell from a fan site dedicated to the Robins, Babe Herman had been a heck of a hitter but a terrible base runner and fielder, so bad he sometimes got hit on the head trying to catch fly balls in the outfield. So much for the bat being worth a fortune.

There was more on the site, but Uncle Dave came back in eating a cup of yogurt. Snider closed the browser so Dave wouldn't see him getting too into it.

"So, um, I think this bat might have belonged to Babe Herman, this guy who played for Brooklyn a long time ago."

Dave filed some paperwork in a wooden file cabinet. "How do you figure that?" he asked.

"Well, it's got his name stamped on it."

Dave nodded but didn't look up. "Could be a factory bat. One of those models they sell at the store so you can own the same bat as your favorite major leaguer. Nobody's going to pay more than what you put on that sheet. Dig deeper."

"*Dig deeper,*" Snider muttered under his breath. "Dig you a *grave.*"

"What's that?" Dave asked from across the room.

"I'm digging away," Snider covered. He turned back to the computer. There were lots of hits for baseball almanac sites and statistical pages, and a few mentions of Babe Herman on websites built by middle-aged dudes who got all teary-eyed about the good old days of baseball at Ebbets Field. More than once he read about Herman doubling into a double play, when he and two other Robins ended up all standing on third base at the same time. The guy sounded like an idiot, but these website guys loved him. Maybe the bat could be worth something to one of these jokers after all.

The best stuff about Herman and the Robins was written

by a guy named John Kieran in the *New York Times*. From the looks of it he wrote about all kinds of New York sports from back in the day, but he seemed to really enjoy laying into the Robins. His stuff was hysterical: He'd start off with poetic stuff, then find some way to slam the team before the end of the first paragraph. The trouble was, that's all Snider could read for free. The rest of the articles cost money to read, and there was no way he was doing that.

Besides, how would any of it prove Babe Herman had actually used this bat? He was about to give up when he read the first paragraph of a Kieran story that started off with a description of Babe Herman stepping up to the plate, talking about how he spit a huge glop of tobacco juice on his hands and rubbed it all over the bat's handle. The brown stains! Snider sniffed the bat. Was that a faint tobacco smell? Maybe that stuff wasn't pine tar, maybe it was tobacco—which was actually pretty gross. The question was, were they Babe Herman's tobacco stains?

The article also said Herman knocked the dirt off his cleats with the bat, and Snider knew exactly what Kieran was talking about. He'd done that to his own cleats a thousand times playing on the Prospect Park fields, only his bat was graphite and indestructible. Well, except that it had melted with everything else in the fire. But smacking his shoes with it had never done any damage to it, not like it would have done to a wooden bat, and Herman would have had metal cleats that really chewed it up.

Snider stood and hopped until he was balanced on his one good leg, then took the wooden bat in hand and pretended to knock dirt off the bottom of his cast. The chewed-up part was perfectly placed.

Snider lost his balance and the bat slipped. It *thwacked* his cast and he yowled.

"Everything okay in there?" Uncle Dave asked. Snider noticed he didn't exactly come running.

"Yeah, great," Snider said. He winced and sat back down, leaning the bat against the counter.

The stamps on the handle were the next thing Snider had to figure out. Who would put postage stamps on a bat and drop it in a mailbox, and why? He did a couple of searches with Babe Herman and stamps, then just with stamps and bats, but got nothing useful either way—just more stuff about Babe Ruth and stamp collecting. But a stamp collector might be able to tell him something about the pieces on the bat, right? They put new stamps out every year. Maybe some stamp nut could tell him at least what year the bat was mailed.

Snider tried his uncle first, figuring he might know something since he owned an antiques store, but Dave shook his head.

"Not my thing," he said through a mouthful of granola bar. "You need a philatelist."

"A whatsit?"

"Stamp collector."

No duh, Snider thought. Dave went to an old paper Rolodex file and pulled out a card. "Here's the guy I send people to when they come in with stamps. He's here in Brooklyn."

Snider snagged a packing tube to carry the bat in and told Dave he was going out, checking the time on his phone to make sure he would get back in time to watch the Mets game that evening. A short subway ride later Snider was *thunking* his way down a sidewalk in Williamsburg, looking for the address of "Philo's Philately." He shuddered to think what his friends would say if they heard about *this.*

The stamp shop was on the top floor of a two-story walk-up that put his iffy crutch skills to the test, and Snider wondered, not for the first time that day, if any of this was even worth it. At the top of the stairs he paused to catch his breath, then rang the bell.

Philo—if that was really the dude's name—was a small, wiry man with thick glasses, a tall, thin neck, and a balding head. Everything about him was brown too—he had brown eyes, brown hair, brown corduroy pants, a brown collared shirt, and a brown sweater. He raised a suspicious eyebrow at Snider, the same kind of look Snider had seen on the faces of countless adults who wondered what kind of trouble a fourteen-year-old boy was about to bring them. Snider was tempted to just turn around and forget about it, but he'd already come all this way.

"Yes?"

"My name is Snider Flint. I'm David Flint's nephew. He sent me with a question about philly—philata—with a question about some stamps."

Uncle Dave's name worked like a magical key, and the brown man opened the door wide for Snider. "Ah. Mr. Flint has sent a great deal of business my way. Philo Cohen," he said by way of introduction. "How can I be of assistance?"

The inside of Philo's Philately was as brown as its owner, filled with dark wood chairs and tables and stained brown bookcases filled with brown-covered books. There was nothing brown about the insides of the display cases throughout the room, though. They were filled with every color of the rainbow, all in tiny inch-tall works of art.

"Sorry," Snider said when he realized he hadn't answered Philo's question.

"Not at all. Postage stamps are my passion, and too often I forget how *dazzling* they can be when one is not surrounded by them all the time."

"Ah, yeah. Right."

"Now, how may I help, Master Flint?"

Snider put the packing tube on a table and withdrew the baseball bat. Philo arched an eyebrow, but understood when Snider turned the handle to reveal the postage stamp fragments.

"Intriguing," said Philo. He beckoned Snider to bring the bat over to another table with a lamp and a magnifying glass on swinging arms.

"Why on earth would someone put postage stamps on a baseball bat?"

"No idea," Snider said. "And I know they're kind of torn up, but I was hoping you could at least tell me what year they came out."

Philo studied the bat handle under a powerful magnifying glass.

"Snider is an interesting name," Philo said.

"What?"

"Your first name. Is it a family name?"

"Yeah. It's like the last name of a whole other side of my family."

"Aha!"

"Aha?"

Philo pointed to one of the stamps under the glass with a pair of tweezers. "This one will be the thirteen-cent Harrison." He chuckled. "A makeup stamp. Postmaster New was a Benjamin Harrison man. Resented Woodrow Wilson getting a seventeen-cent stamp the year before."

"Yeah, I can see how he would hate that," Snider said, not really having any idea what the guy was talking about.

"And here, this one . . . torn, but obviously a two-cent Sesquicentennial Exposition stamp. You can even see the gum breakers here on the back where it's peeled up a bit—"

"That's great," Snider said. "But can you tell me what year the stamps came out?"

Philo Cohen stood. "Well, a sesquicentennial is one hundred and fifty years. That means this stamp was printed for the one hundred and fiftieth anniversary of the United States."

Snider glanced around for a calculator.

"1926," Philo said.

"1926? You're sure?"

Philo selected a brown volume off the shelf, flipped through a few pages, and turned it so Snider could see it. There, under the exciting heading "Postage Stamps of the United States First Issued in 1926" were full-color pictures that matched the torn pieces of the two stamps still clinging to the bat.

"Hey, that's great!" Snider said. "Can I get a copy of that page?"

Philo bowed slightly. "I'm happy to oblige. If you'll wait just a moment."

While the philatelist went to a photocopier in his office, Snider peered through the magnifying glass at the stamps. He turned the bat to see the stamp fragments better and saw again the illegible handwritten address. Under a bright light and a magnifying glass it wasn't so illegible.

"Spalding, Chicago, Illinois?"

Philo returned from his office. "What's that?"

"The address. It just says, 'Spalding, Chicago, Illinois.'"

"You'd be surprised at how diligent the U.S. Postal Service is about delivering to even the vaguest of addresses," Philo told him, "and people were far less careful about those things in the past, from what I've seen on vintage envelopes."

"But who is Spalding? I know I've seen that name just recently."

"If I may?" Philo said, turning the bat slightly. There, clear as day under the magnifying glass, was written in the bat's baseball diamond logo: "Trade Mark Spalding No. 200, Oil Temp. Made in U.S.A."

So the bat had been mailed back to its maker in 1926, and Snider was pretty sure Babe Herman had used the bat himself. So why had he sent it back to the bat company? And how could Snider prove it was Herman who sent it?

Snider thanked Philo and escaped before the philatelist could tell him the story of every single postage stamp on the premises. But instead of heading back to Fulton Street Antiques and Collectibles, Snider took the subway to Grand Army Plaza to hit the Brooklyn Public Library. John Kieran had steered him right the first time, and he wanted to go back and see what else the writer could tell him. With a year now—1926, Babe Herman's rookie year—a librarian was able to help Snider find everything John Kieran had written about the Brooklyn Nine for the entire year. Then he had to sit at a huge microfiche machine and scroll through every *New York Times* for that year until he got to the articles he wanted—but at least it was free. Still, it would have driven him nuts if Kieran wasn't as funny as the guys on ESPN.

Snider read for almost an hour until he found it, the last piece of the puzzle about Babe Herman's bat. It was so perfect he almost shouted out loud. In an interview with John Kieran just a few days after the infamous double/double play, Babe Herman told the reporter with a completely straight face that he didn't blame himself, or his teammates, or even the umpires. He blamed his bat. It had to be flawed—that was the only answer to his recent struggles. The bat was defective, he figured, and that very day he had marched down to the post office and mailed the cursed thing back to the fellows who'd made it.

3

Uncle Dave munched on a carrot while he read through the photocopied pages Snider had laid out.

"Is it good enough?"

"You mean, does it prove this was really Babe Herman's bat? Yeah, I'd say so."

Snider nodded with what he hoped wasn't too much enthusiasm.

Uncle Dave examined the bat. "Better than that, you've proven this bat was used on a particular day, in a particular game. A *famous* game, no less. A provenance like this without an eyewitness is practically impossible. This is really impressive, Snider."

"What do you think it's worth?"

Uncle Dave took a bite out of his carrot.

"I don't know. Say . . . twelve hundred dollars?"

"Twelve. Hundred. Dollars!?"

"Just an educated guess, really. Collectible value is all about what the market will bear."

Snider pulled a calculator over and did the math. His commission on $1,200 would be $180. That was six tickets in the upper deck box seats at Shea Stadium. He rubbed his hands together.

"Okay, so now what?"

"Now we wait and see if someone's looking for a Babe Herman bat. We'll put it on display here in the shop and we'll list it online."

Snider's heart sank as he looked around the cluttered shop. Most of this stuff had been here as long as he could remember.

"So what am I supposed to do in the meantime?"

"Go back to the box. See what you can do with everything else. That baseball has to have a story."

Uncle Dave went to the computer to list the bat and Snider slumped on his stool. There had to be some way of finding a buyer quicker than just putting the thing up in the front window or waiting for someone to type "Babe Herman bat" into a search engine. He tossed up the ratty old ball from the box and caught it. He didn't know the ball's story, but the bat had a story. The trick was just figuring out who cared enough about that story to buy it.

Those fan sites. That's who cared enough to buy it—whoever took the time to post those websites Snider had found when he first searched online for info about Babe Herman and the Brooklyn Robins. When Dave was finished at the computer Snider hopped over and found the sites again. A couple of them hadn't been updated in a while, but one had a photo gallery with new pics added in the last six months, and it even had a forum where people could discuss their memories. There were very few posts—most of them by the host. That was the guy Snider wanted.

Snider wrote an e-mail introducing himself and giving a little background on the bat. He didn't want to go too overboard, though, in case the guy wasn't interested, and he didn't want it to sound like spam either. He read over the e-mail one more time, then hit SEND and went back to the box of baseball memorabilia. All morning long he tried every angle he could think of to find out more about the hat, the photo, the beauty guide, and particularly the baseball. Nothing. He even got the phone number of the Atlanta auction company Uncle Dave had bought the lot from and called to see if they could put him in touch with the original owner. They couldn't. The box had been part of an estate sale: Some man named Walker who had no close relations for Snider to call.

It was crazy to think the guy who ran the Brooklyn Robins site would e-mail him back that day—or ever—but Snider kept checking. Why not? He didn't have anything better to do. But it was more than that now. He'd come all this way and he wanted to see it out, to finish it.

And a hundred eighty bucks wouldn't be too bad either.

Snider was reading about how early baseballs were made when the e-mail alert chimed and he clicked over to find a response from the man with the Robins site. He was interested! He wanted to see the bat! His name was Brian McNamara, he was a teacher in New Jersey, and he wanted to come to Brooklyn later tonight—but it would be after the store was already closed. Snider called Uncle Dave in and showed him the e-mail.

"Tell him I'll keep the store open, and you'll be here to talk to him."

"Me?"

"Sure. It's your commission, right? This is your deal. That means you make the sale."

"What do I do? What do I say?"

"Tell him everything you told me. Show him all the research you collected on the bat. If he's interested, negotiate a price. Start at one thousand five hundred dollars, though. He'll want to haggle. And I know you know how to haggle."

Uncle Dave went back to work and Snider hit REPLY, but his hands hovered over the keyboard. He suddenly wasn't so sure he wanted to sell the thing, which was stupid. It was just a dumb old bat, right?

Mr. McNamara was a white-haired man, older than Uncle Dave but not grandfatherly, with a neatly trimmed white beard and an easygoing smile. True to his word, Uncle Dave sat back and watched while Snider laid out his research for the man. At first Snider was nervous and stumbled over the points he had spent all afternoon preparing, but McNamara listened patiently.

"May I hold it?" he asked when Snider was finished.

Snider looked to his uncle to see if it was all right, but all Dave did was smile.

"Sure, I guess," Snider said.

McNamara took the bat in his hands as though he were weighing it. He ran his hands down the length of it, pausing to feel the indentions where the Spalding logo had been burned on. He felt the chewed-up end, examined the torn postage stamps, smelled the handle, and Snider felt another pang at maybe parting with it.

"Can you imagine?" he said. "The very same bat Babe Herman used to hit that double off the wall in right center. They say he was such an incredible hitter that they had to put a fence on top of the right field wall at Ebbets to keep him from putting out the windows of the building across the street. I don't remember the fence, but then I didn't get to see many games at Ebbets before the Dodgers left town. My father took me to the very last game they ever played there in 1957. I was very young, but I can still remember the grown men and women weeping around me at the end."

Snider had a hard time picturing a stadium full of adults crying about a baseball team leaving town, but he didn't say anything.

"The provenance was your work, I take it?" the man asked Snider.

"Yes sir."

"It's a fabulous piece of detective work. How much are you asking?"

"One—one thousand five hundred dollars," Snider said, his voice cracking. He'd meant to be so much firmer about that, but the weird feeling he had about not wanting to sell it made him stumble.

The older man set the bat back on the counter and stared at it. Snider could tell he wanted it. But did he want it more than Snider did? How much would this guy pay for a piece of history, a mere piece of wood that had value far beyond the material used to make it?

"I'll give you one thousand dollars," the man said.

One thousand dollars! It wasn't what they had wanted to get, but a thousand dollars was a lot of money. Snider looked back at his uncle, but Dave just shrugged at him, as if to say: "It's your deal."

Snider cleared his throat. "Fourteen hundred."

"Eleven."

"Thirteen," Snider said, falling into the negotiation more easily now.

"Twelve hundred—and I'm afraid that's as high as I can go."

"Done," Snider said. *Twelve hundred dollars!* He'd sold the bat for twelve hundred dollars.

McNamara visibly relaxed, then smiled. "He's quite good at this, you know," he said to Uncle Dave, who had come over to handle the payment.

"His first find," Dave said. "He's a natural."

Snider stood with Mr. McNamara while Dave ran his credit card. It was gone. The bat he'd worked so hard to document, Babe Herman's bat, wasn't his anymore. The white-haired man put his hand on it again.

"Oh, this was an extravagance," he said, "but I had to buy it. For my father. He was there, you know. At the game where Herman ended up on third base with Fewster and Vance. He used to tell me stories about the Daffiness Boys when I was young."

"Are you going to give the bat to him, then?" Snider asked.

"Oh no. He's dead now. For the last few years he didn't even remember who I was, but he remembered the Dodgers, the Robins, all those games he went to as a boy. It was the only thing we could really talk about, the only connection we still had." He smiled sadly. "I suppose that's all we ever have in the end. Stories about the people who are gone and a few mementos to remind us they were here."

McNamara settled up and said his good-byes, and Uncle Dave locked the front door and turned off the lights.

"You did it," he said.

"Yeah."

Uncle Dave opened the cash register and counted out one hundred and eighty dollars. "Your commission," he said.

Snider fanned out the money, not so much to count it as to look at it.

"You wish you hadn't sold it?" his uncle asked.

"A little. Yeah."

"That happens. You became part of its story, if only for a few days. That's not easy to let go of. But you didn't have to sell it."

"I know," Snider said. He put the money in his pocket and worked himself up on to his crutches. "But that guy should have it. That bat was a bigger part of his life. It meant more to him than it did to me."

"You mean like your old house meant a lot more to me and your dad than it does to you?"

"Yeah, yeah, yeah. I get it. Beat me over the head with it, why don't you."

Uncle Dave raised his hands in surrender. "I'm just saying. All right. So, you think you can pull any more miracles out of that box?"

"Nah. I've been over this stuff a hundred times. There's a Sandy Koufax card worth maybe forty bucks, and this Jim Gilliam guy is worth like ten or fifteen, but there's no special story for either one of them. This Brooklyn cap is vintage—worth maybe a few hundred dollars—but I don't know who wore it or when. And I don't know who's going to want a photo of some Little League championship team from Long Island."

Uncle Dave pulled the tattered old brown baseball out of the box. "What about this?"

Snider took the ball from him. "Well, it's old. Like early eighteen hundreds old, based on the way it's stitched. It was handmade too—you can see the holes poked through are uneven, and the leather flaps aren't exactly the same size. And this piece—see underneath it?—there's some wear *inside* the ball, like this is leather from a shoe or something. Maybe the person who made it was a tailor or a shoemaker or something. I don't know. Only thing I know for sure is that somebody really loved this ball."

"What makes you say that?"

"Look at it. It got used so much it fell apart, and every time it fell apart somebody repaired it again, over and over. They even carved their initial into it too—*S*."

Dave took the ball from Snider. "You couldn't figure out anything else about it?"

Snider shrugged. "I called the people who sold it. It was part of some guy's estate, but he's dead now, and there wasn't anyone left who was related to him. If he knew what its deal was, where it came from, it died with him. But it had to have some kind of story. Why else would anybody keep a junky old ball like this around?"

"Sentimental value," Dave said.

"Yeah. Which means it's worthless, I guess."

"Not to the person who kept it all those years," his uncle said. "And not to you. Here. You keep it. It's yours."

"But it's old. It has to be worth *something.*"

"Okay. Give me ten bucks for it."

"Five," Snider said.

Uncle Dave laughed. "Deal. You drive a hard bargain, especially when you could have had it for free." He made change for Snider from the till. "There. Now it's official. You're part of its history. 'Purchased by Snider Flint in Brooklyn, New York, June 13, 2002.' There's just the small issue of a hundred-fifty-year gap in the provenance." He grinned. "But from now on, you'll know exactly what its story is, because you'll be living it."

Snider ran his fingers over the rough seams of the ball and brushed the carved letter S with his thumb—an S for Snider now.

"I wonder what happened to the guy who made this?"

Uncle Dave turned off the last of the lights. "There's no telling. Come on—there's a Mets game on TV, and I think I know where the remote is."

Author Notes

First Inning

Alexander Cartwright, considered by many today to be the father of modern baseball, was a bookseller and volunteer fireman, and his Knickerbocker Volunteer Fire Department gave its name to the baseball club Cartwright helped found. For their new sport, the Knickerbockers borrowed rules from older ball games like "town ball," "three-out, all-out," and "one old cat," and added some new rules of their own—like standard distances between the bases, foul territory, and, most importantly, no more throwing the ball at runners ("soaking" them) to get them out! In 1849 Cartwright left New York and, like so many other people, headed for California to try and get rich in the gold rush. He introduced the Knickerbocker baseball rules to towns and players all along the way, becoming a sort of Johnny Appleseed of America's game.

Second Inning

Contrary to popular belief, Abner Doubleday, who makes an appearance this inning as a real Union general, did not invent the game of baseball in a cow pasture in Cooperstown, New York. That myth was most likely started by sports-star-turned-sporting-goods-manufacturer Albert G. Spalding, who was desperate to convince the world that baseball was an American invention with no ties to older games or other countries. Despite zero evidence that Doubleday had ever even *seen* a baseball, much less invented the game, the idea was presented as fact, a Hall of Fame was built in Cooperstown, and the myth persists to this day.

Third Inning

As professional baseball became the national pastime, Mike "King" Kelly became one of its first great stars. A true showman, Kelly really did travel with a Japanese manservant and a pet monkey, and he is thought to be the first ballplayer to give autographs and the first to sell the rights to his name and image for product advertising. The song "Slide, Kelly, Slide" became a nationwide hit when it was released on a phonograph cylinder by Edison Studios, and after his playing career Kelly traded in on his fame to star on the vaudeville stage. In many ways, though, Kelly's story is as sad as that of the slugger in "Casey at the Bat." Heavy drinking cut short Kelly's playing career and his life. Already washed out of professional baseball, Kelly died when he was just thirty-six years old.

The title of this story comes from the subtitle of Ernest Thayer's "Casey at the Bat: A Ballad of the Republic," which was published in the *San Francisco Examiner* in 1888.

Fourth Inning

Hall of Famer Cyclone Joe Williams (later known as Smokey Joe Williams) was perhaps the greatest pitcher of his era, black or white, even though he never played a day in the majors. As far as I know, Cyclone Joe never tried to pass himself off as a Native American, but one black man during that time *did*. In 1901, Baltimore Orioles manager John McGraw tried to sign black second baseman Charlie Grant to a major league contract as an American Indian named Chief Tokohama. McGraw and Grant were busted before "Tokohama" could ever play a game, and baseball's color barrier remained unbroken for another forty-six years.

Fifth Inning

The 1920s were the heyday of wordy, "purple prose" sports writing, and John Kieran was one of its most famous figures. Kieran wrote for the *New York Times* sports section for almost thirty years, filling his sports columns with references to Latin, law, poetry, nature, and the works of William Shakespeare. In the hours before ball games, Kieran could be found visiting museums, zoos, parks, and libraries, and he had a habit of writing his articles in advance of the actual games. While I can't say that Kieran ever really conspired to fix a numbers game, he certainly seems like the kind of man who would have appreciated the effort.

One of Kieran's favorite subjects had to have been Babe Herman, who led the league in errors, put lit cigars in his pockets, twice stopped to watch long home runs while running the base paths only to be passed by the hitter and called out, and really did double into a double play. A teammate of Babe Herman said, "He wore a glove for one reason: Because it was a league custom." Years later during World War II when many of the younger players were called to military service, Herman was brought out of retirement to play for the Dodgers. He singled in his first at bat but tripped over first base and was almost thrown out. The Brooklyn fans gave him a standing ovation.

Sixth Inning

The All-American Girls Softball League was founded in 1943 by Chicago Cubs owner Phillip Wrigley, who wanted a women's league that would play in major league stadiums while the men's teams were on the road. The league played a cross between softball and baseball until the end of the 1945 season, when the name was changed to the All-American Girls Professional Baseball League, and overhand pitching and smaller ball sizes were adopted. Almost 200,000 fans turned out during the first season to watch the women play ball, and even though Wrigley's dream of women playing to packed major league stadiums never did happen, the league lived on in small Midwestern towns until 1954, when the AAGPBL played its last skirted season.

All the major characters in this story besides Kat—from the players to the coach to the ball girl—were real people.

Seventh Inning

Duck and Cover was an educational film shown to American schoolkids, and, at least at the time I write this, can be seen in its entirety on both Wikipedia and YouTube. Years later, people argued that ducking and covering would provide little real help in the event of a nuclear attack, and that the film did nothing but heighten kids' fears. That didn't stop the film from being shown over and over again to students from the late 1940s all the way, incredibly, to the 1980s.

Eighth Inning

As of the beginning of the 2008 season, there have been only seventeen official perfect games in the history of Major League Baseball. More people have orbited the moon than thrown perfect games in the majors, and no pitcher has ever thrown more than one. The ninth inning of Michael's perfect game in my story is loosely based on the ninth inning of the perfect game thrown by Sandy Koufax of the Los Angeles Dodgers in 1965. I've tried to evoke the poetry of Dodgers radio announcer Vin Scully's call of that game in my story, including a nod to my favorite line from his broadcast: "I would think that the mound at Dodger Stadium right now is the loneliest place in the world." The brief but thrilling transcript of Scully's ninth-inning call of Sandy Koufax's perfect game can be found online.

Ninth Inning

In 2006, a Babe Herman Pro Model Signature Bat was sold to a collector at auction for $1,508. Tobacco stains and cleat marks proved it had been used in games, but there is no way to know if it was the same bat Herman used to hit into the famous double/double play. Oddly, the bat does bear the remnants of three postage stamps on the barrel, and faint, illegible writing that may be the address of Spalding, the bat's manufacturer. How or why the bat was mailed back to the factory no one knows.

Extra Innings

The story of the Gratzes is not nearly as exciting as the story of the Schneiders and Flints, but my own family history played a part for me in the writing of this novel.

Our family's American journey began in 1861, when nineteen-year-old Louis Alexander Gratz, a German Jew, landed in New York City with ten dollars in his pockets and no knowledge of English. A few months later he volunteered to fight in the Civil War, and less than a year after arriving in America, Louis Gratz was an officer in the Union Army. Louis, the main character in "The Red-Legged Devil" is named in his honor.

Though Louis Gratz never changed his last name, he did,

like some immigrant Jews, convert to Christianity to better fit in. Louis covered his tracks so well, in fact, that my family didn't even know we had Jewish ancestors until my grandfather began to research our family history more than a hundred years later!

To help research the Seventh Inning, I interviewed my father, who was a boy in 1957. He remembers duck and cover drills and collecting baseball cards when he was a kid. I was able to draw on my own childhood for the Eighth Inning, when I played youth baseball and worshipped movies like *Star Wars* and *Raiders of the Lost Ark*.

By 2002, I had grown up and moved away from home and had a family of my own, but still not a day goes by during baseball season that I don't talk to my father on the phone about some terrific hit, some great defensive play, or the sad state of the fantasy baseball team we share. Baseball, more than any other sport, has a magical way of connecting fathers and sons, mothers and daughters, grandparents and grandchildren, and ancestors back down the line. For that reason and many more, *The Brooklyn Nine* is, at long last, dedicated to my mom and dad.

Special Thanks

I owe a great debt of thanks for *The Brooklyn Nine* to editor extraordinaire Liz Waniewski—not to be confused with Grand Rapids Chicks pitcher Connie Wisniewski, although I more than once typed "Liz" instead of "Connie" in that inning. Editorial thanks are also due to Brad Anderson, who got his first big-league at bats against me, and Robyn Meshulam, who led the team in assists. And thanks as always to copy editor Regina Castillo, who of course bats cleanup.

In an age when information is a commodity, we're incredibly lucky to still have libraries where all that wonderful knowledge is free for the asking, and I am indebted to the libraries of Emory University, the University of Tennessee, Knoxville, and Appalachian State University for the bulk of the research I did on this book. I routinely cleared out their baseball and American history shelves for this project, and any mistakes that remain are my own.

And thanks of course to my wife, Wendi, and my daughter, Jo, who put up with my surly editing moods, my closed office door, and baseball on TV every night, and special thanks to all the Gratzes, past and present; I am just another chapter in your story.

Be sure to read Alan Gratz's

SAMURAI SHORTSTOP

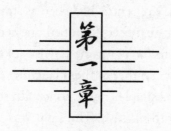

Chapter One

TOYO WATCHED carefully as his uncle prepared to kill himself.

Before dawn, he had swept and cleaned his uncle's favorite shrine, down to polishing the small mirror that hung on a post at its center. When that was done, he carefully arranged new *tatami* mats on the dirt floor. Everything had to be perfect for Uncle Koji's *seppuku*.

Now Toyo sat in the damp grass outside the shrine as his uncle moved to the center of the mats. Uncle Koji's face was a mask of calm. He wore a ceremonial white kimono with brilliant red wings—the wings he usually wore only into battle. He was clean-shaven and recently bathed, and he wore his hair in a tight topknot like the samurai of old. Uncle Koji knelt on the tatami mats keeping his hands on his hips and his arms akimbo.

Toyo's father, Sotaro, crouched next to Koji. Though older than his brother, Toyo's father was slightly smaller, with a long, thin face and a sharp nose like a *katana* blade. They used to joke that Koji's nose had been as straight as his older brother's, until it had been flattened one too many times in judo practice. But today was no day for jokes. In fact, Toyo couldn't remember either of them laughing for a long time.

Sotaro wore a simple gray kimono with the family swords tucked neatly into his sash. The sight was strange to Toyo. For as long as he could remember, the katana and *wakizashi* had been retired to a place of honor in their home. Carrying them outside like this was illegal, though his father would soon be using the swords to carry out an order signed by the emperor himself.

Uncle Koji bowed to Toyo, the ceremony's other witness. Returning the bow from his knees, Toyo touched his head to the ground to show his great respect for his uncle. His father nodded, and Toyo stood and picked up a small wooden stand supporting a short sword about as long as his forearm. The point and the edge of the blade were razor sharp. Toyo strained to keep his legs from shaking as he entered the shrine. Kneeling a little clumsily, he bowed low to the ground once more to present the short wakizashi to his uncle.

When he felt the weight of the sword lift from the stand, Toyo looked up at Koji. His uncle held the wakizashi cradled in his hands as though it were a newborn child. Uncle Koji closed his eyes, touched the flat part of the blade to his forehead, and set the wakizashi in front of him on the mat. He gave a quick smile then for Toyo, the same grin he always flashed right before getting them into trouble.

Instead of making him feel better, the grin deepened Toyo's sense of panic. He didn't want to lose his uncle.

2

Throughout all the preparations, he had fought to focus on something else—anything else. His first day of school at Ichiko tomorrow, his coming sixteenth birthday, even baseball. But when this ceremony was finished his uncle would be dead and gone. Forever. None of his strength, none of his compassion, none of his spirit would remain.

Toyo backed away, unable to meet Uncle Koji's eyes.

"For my part in the samurai uprising at Ueno Park," his uncle said officially, "I, Koji Shimada, have been sentenced to die. The emperor, in his divine graciousness, has granted me the honor of committing seppuku rather than die at the hands of his executioner. I beg those present here today to bear witness to my death."

Uncle Koji bowed low, and Sotaro and Toyo bowed in return.

He slowly untied the sash around his waist and loosened the kimono wrapped underneath. Pulling the stiff shirt down off his shoulders, Koji exposed his smooth round belly. He tucked the arms of the kimono under his legs, which made him lean forward. Toyo knew this was to help his uncle pitch forward if he should pass out during the ceremony. It would make his father's job much easier.

Uncle Koji closed his eyes and began the poem he had written for the occasion of his death:

> "In the darkness after the earthquake,
> The Flowers of Edo burn bright and fast—
> Only to be replaced in the morning
> By the light of a new day."

When he was finished, the samurai opened his eyes and put his hands on his stomach, almost as if he were saying good-bye to it. Then Koji took the short sword in his hands and turned the blade toward his gut.

"Brother," Koji said, "please wait until I have finished my task."

"*Hai.*" Toyo's father nodded.

Koji looked past Toyo then, past the little path to the shrine, past the line of trees that circled the clearing. Whether he saw something in the distance or not, Toyo didn't know, but the faraway look stayed in his uncle's eyes as he plunged the wakizashi into his belly. Blood covered his hands and his jaw locked tight, but Koji held his grip on the sword, dragging it across his stomach from left to right. Toyo fought the urge to look away. To honor his promise to bear witness, he forced himself to watch as his uncle's insides spilled onto the floor of the Shinto shrine, the body deflating like a torn rice sack.

When Uncle Koji had sliced all the way across his stomach, he turned the wakizashi in the wound and pulled it diagonally up through his chest. Never flinching, his eyes remained steady and resolute. The knife reached his heart, and with the last of his strength Uncle Koji pulled the wakizashi out, laid it by his side, and fell forward on his hands and knees.

Toyo's father sprang to his feet, raising the long katana blade high over his head.

"*Heeeeeeeeeeeiaaaaaaaaaaaa!*" Sotaro cried. He brought the blade down with blinding speed and chopped Koji's head clean off his body.

4